A SNEAKY INC. SPY ADVENTURE

OPERATION
DEEP BLACK

BOOK 4

I0631701

CHRISTIAN
ACTION BOOKS
FOR UPPER MIDDLE
GRADE & TEENS

ROB BADDORF

ISBN: 978-1-968391-01-0

RobBaddorf.com

SELAH

Therefore we will not fear,
    though the earth give way
    and the mountains fall
    into the heart of the sea.
    Psalm 46:2 (NIV)

———

Trust in the Lord with all your heart
    and lean not on your own understanding;
    in all your ways submit to him,
    and he will make your paths straight.
    Proverbs 3:5–6 (NIV)

1

obin tied the laces on his new pair of black boots. Supple leather, hand-stitched. Expensive. Maybe a bit of a luxury item considering their moderate budget.

He tilted his head way back and gazed upward. Why was *he* here, exactly? Out of all his teammates, none of whom seemed to have an issue with heights . . .

Why did Robin have this job specifically?!

On top of an already-large rise sat an even taller cell tower.

Robin frowned.

He could feel the effects already. Coursing through his veins. Pumping a low level of adrenaline even before he had touched the first rung of the ladder.

"Lord, will you take away my fear of heights?" Robin whispered. "I mean, once and for all. A complete healing would be nice."

He hesitated a moment.

Looking for a quick response, maybe. An instant solution.

Waiting for the icy tingle in his body to miraculously vanish.

"Right about now would be perfect."

But it didn't. Nothing changed.

Robin adjusted the straps on his ram-air parachute. It was only for backup. A safety feature just in case. Robin had insisted on it. And for some reason, he wanted the backpack to hug him tighter. To be a little closer and to reassure him that what he was about to do wasn't completely and utterly stupid.

Which it was.

No, no, it wasn't stupid. He needed to stop thinking that way. Stinking thinking! The work before him was simply part of the job.

If he didn't like it, there was always Burger Barn. As far as he knew, they were still hiring. They pretty much always needed workers to drop the onion rings into the vats of hot oil. Someone to flip the burgers. To wrap the sandwiches, hot off the grill, in precut sheets of wax paper.

And right now, all of those positions were looking attractive again.

Why had he ever left working there?

Robin swallowed hard.

Gripping the first metal peg on the tower, he took the first step up.

See, that wasn't so bad.

He could do this.

It wasn't an issue.

Now all he had to do was about a thousand more.

Rung after rung, Robin climbed.

He quieted his mind. Tried to focus.

Only on the next rung.

Then one more.

Repeat.

Had his father ever done this? Climbed a tower like this one?

How interesting would it be if Robin's dad had climbed this very tower?!

Not likely. Robin still struggled to see his father as anything more than an accountant. A number-cruncher. A guy who lived in the land of spreadsheets and data.

Gripping the next rung, Robin pressed on. Ever higher.

Apparently, some trickster above him was stealing phone data. Likely a set of local hackers looking for a good time. That's why Robin and his team were called in. A low security concern, as their bosses put it. Yet here Robin was. Climbing the stairway to heaven to see what he could find at the top. The hackers had likely flown a drone up and switched out a few wires. On the ground, Anika and Chad were handling the other half of the equation. Ha. They had the easy part!

That's when Robin spied it.

The sun setting. Inching ever lower. The rays of warm light subtly changing directions. Illuminating the same things but in a new way.

And the brilliant display was now smack-dab in front of him.

He could hardly miss it. Unless all he was capable of was staring at what was inches away from his nose.

Amazing!

Simply stunning. A long expanse of salmon and indigo clouds streaked the sky. And with every rung of the cold metal ladder he ascended, it only got better. More real.

A flock of blackbirds cawed and flew by. Who could really make something like this? Inspire such an amazing and grandiose spectacle that—

Robin missed a rung!

His hand had simply grasped too far to one side. Reaching out, he grabbed nothing!

Robin froze. Stabilized himself. Acid flooding his gut!

3

Liquid ice coursing through his veins!

No! He couldn't afford to take in the sights. Not now. Maybe never!

FOCUS!

Robin forced his eyes to open again.

He willed his hands to ease up. To relent in their controlling, vicelike grip.

More. A little more.

He reached for the next rung and gripped it genuinely, feeling the metal through his gloves. Its solid reality pressed up against his own. His feet adorned with his new boots followed suit, finding safe purchase.

He stepped up.

Then he repeated it all.

His pace slowly increased.

"Lord, please just keep me from falling off this crazy thing, will ya?"

And he heard it.

Almost like the gentle breeze in the air.

No more than a whisper. *I am always with you, Robin. And I always will be. Even when I am silent.*

Just hearing the words was reassuring.

He knew this. Knew this deep down, but sometimes just hearing it *once* more did wonders for the soul. And had Robin maybe forgotten it? Just a little?

I don't always heal, the whisper continued. *Because I want you reliant on me.*

Robin grimaced. As much as he liked the first words of encouragement, he didn't so much like the second part.

Reach. Grab. Climb.

Robin didn't know if it was worth arguing with a statement like that.

Reach. Grab. Climb.

Mostly because it did kind of contain maybe the smallest morsel of truth.

Reach. Grab. Climb.

Okay, maybe more than a morsel.

Fine!

Robin paused to catch his breath. Climbing as high as he already had really took it out of him.

Robin could rely on more than just himself.

Couldn't he?

After all, he didn't exactly have much of a choice in the matter, now did he?!

2

Always babysitting.

And *never* with the cute, cuddly babies!

Anika grumbled inside as she watched Chad do his thing. How exactly did *she* get stuck with him again?!

As talented as the boy was with locks, it forced anyone with him to keep one eye open, strictly tuned to him.

Here they were. In the opulent lobby of The St. Arcadia Hotel. This was hardly a place to play or act goofy. The two of them didn't belong there in the first place!

Anika looked again at all the gold trim. The ornate wood chairs with their plush backing. The large marble fountain in the middle of the cavernous lobby. The sconces on the pillars. Were those actual flames inside them?

This place was way out of Anika's price range. She and her family were used to staying in places closer to a Motel 6. Maybe a Red Roof Inn, if they were feeling extravagant.

Not here.

And Chad had simply marched himself up to the front desk.

Wearing a smudged T-shirt and shorts, dragging a matte-black backpack behind him like it was a pet.

Like somehow he actually belonged here.

Fit in.

A high-school-aged kid who looked like he should still be in middle school, complete with the goofy grin. He wore plastic prescription glasses, likely bought from the limited children's section, and had bent ear tips. Was he born with those? Or had he tugged on them one too many times?

Chad didn't fit in here.

Not even a little!

Especially with all the adults milling about.

In dark suits and silk ties. Designer knee-high dresses and wide-brimmed hats.

"Oh, excuse me," Anika said, shuffling out of a couple's way. She wanted to blend in. To become part of the furniture. To disappear.

She really didn't like this part of the job.

And the embarrassment of being with Chad while doing it.

She was glad it wasn't *her* marching up to the uniformed gentleman behind the large counter.

It didn't even help that Chad had just turned sixteen. Wasn't his voice supposed to have changed by now? Crack? Yet there was no sign of it. A late bloomer.

Anika couldn't help but feel a little bad for him.

For his shorts that were probably hand-me-downs, one size too small. For the constant jokes and teasing Chad got at school. And for the stories he would tell about his experiences at the bus stop.

But it all seemed to roll off the kid.

Like he was oblivious to it.

Anika would have been glad to have some of that strength.

The ability to let everything just roll off her. To have no chinks in her armor, no way for the barbs of life to find their way into the tender insides.

Then again, it was possible Chad was just ignorant.

Tuned out. Lost in his own world.

Chad did seem capable of having full conversations with himself. Even answering his own questions sometimes.

Or was there more to the boy?

A quiet superpower within?

Anika casually moved around a thick pillar to watch Chad in action.

"Hi there!" he said cheerfully to the front desk attendant. "I'm here to visit my aunt. Aunt Whiney, as we like to call her," Chad added as he plopped an elbow onto the counter, which was just a little too tall for him. He stood there like a cowboy ready to order something at the bar.

Anika winced.

A bull in a china shop.

The attendant's eyebrow rose.

It was so difficult to know with Chad. He did the whole God thing. Maybe that went to his head. Made him act so funny. Anika never could fully understand why people did that. Why they went *there* when there was so unreal.

It almost felt like Chad lived somewhere else in his head.

"Of course, that's just what we call her," Chad continued. "Winnipeg Elisabeth Charlene Winters. Phew, they sure don't make 'em like they used to!"

By now, Chad had a small audience that was growing.

A gentleman spooning the complimentary caviar from a silver heating dish stopped to listen.

A woman sipping tea from real china paused.

"No, siree," Chad coughed. "Aunt Whiney was named after

her grandmother. You see, her grandparents were one of the few that actually profited from the California gold rush. No joke. Laundry services, can you believe it? There were so many dirty miners running around back then, her grandparents got a nickel for every pair of long johns they scrubbed. Nothing to it, really, but they got filthy stinking rich by doing it. Pardon the pun."

What was Chad doing?!

He was going off script. Changing the plan!

He was simply supposed to go up to the front desk and ask to visit his aunt on the fourteenth floor. That was it. Short and simple.

Where had this outlandish family history come from?!

"I believe Aunt Whiney told me she was on the fourteenth floor. Up in the nosebleed section, if you will," Chad said, suddenly leaning over the counter and spinning around the thin computer screen for a better view. "Let me see here. Is that correct?"

"I am sorry!" the attendant barked, yanking back the computer monitor. "But I can*not* give out that information."

"Oh, sure." Chad recoiled, lifting his backpack. "I just need to drop off a few medications to her, that's all. Seems like she had a little run-in with your shrimp cocktails last night."

The man in the sharp business suit standing at the hors d'oeuvres stopped serving himself again. With a quick glance around, he set his half-filled plate down, abandoning it.

"Yup, I don't want to get too graphic with something as sensitive as this," Chad continued with a wink and not even a hint of impropriety. "But when nature calls, you run. I'll just go and tend to her myself," he added, slinging his backpack, which rattled with the sound of pills inside bottles, over a shoulder. He started toward the brass elevator doors.

"No! Excuse me, sir!" the attendant yelled after him. "But only patrons of The St. Arcadia Hotel are allowed upstairs!"

Chad acted like he didn't hear, whistling to himself.

And, as he passed, Chad reached into the open lid on one of the heating pans on the side table. With his bare hand! Grabbing a single shrimp, he tossed it high into the air—

And caught it in his open mouth!

With looks of shock and disdain, the other guests cleared a path for him.

Anika shook her head. She scurried around the long way to catch up to her partner, sticking to the edges of the lobby.

Babysitting!

3

sabella adjusted the lever on her seat.

Again!

She simply could not get comfortable with the new table height. Her elbows continued to bump against it.

For that matter, everything felt off. Wrong!

After trying two new levels, she rolled the chair up closer to the bank of glowing monitors before her. That felt better.

Or did it?

Maybe it was the lumbar support in the chair?

Sneaky Inc. had officially graduated from their lawn mowing cover. They even held a party—with a homemade applesauce cake and bubbly grape juice!—to retire the beloved PLANTED trailer. Everyone had thought it was a good idea to sell the command center trailer. With another member on the team and the ever-growing inventory of supplies they needed, it only seemed right to upgrade.

When Isabella found a good deal on Marketplace, she had been the one to push for something bigger. But Isabella was second-guessing all of that now.

. . .

Just a little.

With most of the staff having turned sixteen, or very nearly, it made sense to get something with a motor attached this time. No more having to rely on Uber to drag the lawn care trailer halfway around the world. No. Now, because their truck was under a certain weight, they could drive their mobile command center themselves.

And so buying a well-used food truck only made perfect sense!

Or so it looked on paper.

Reality seemed to want to offer its own opinion.

Isabella held her hands together, bowed her head, and closed her eyes. "Dear Lord Jesus, thank you for today. And um, please let tonight's operation go well. Amen." She opened her eyes and then quickly shut them again. "Oh, and please let the truck's engine start this time, if that's alright with you."

It had been a year now. But in some ways, she still felt like a new Christian. Were postscripts allowed in prayer? Or did you need to start all over and log it in as a whole new prayer with the proper opening and closing?

Okay, she had to get down to work again.

And she did. Focusing on the left screen and the sensor readout.

From everything she could tell, what they were looking for was still in the hotel.

Someone was playing with the local cellular connection. Hacking into it.

Not that anyone using their phones would know. It had been a seamless crossover. But illegal. Likely stealing data from unsuspecting users.

It certainly wasn't the most exciting operation. But with the lack of excitement usually came a level of safety that Isabella was glad for.

From his GPS tracker, Isabella could see Robin was still at the tower. He was on assignment to find the point of access.

Anika and Chad were inside the hotel, looking for the source of the copycat signal. When—

KNOCK, KNOCK.

Hold up. Isabella's hands hovered over the keyboard, frozen.

KNOCK, KNOCK.

This wasn't actually happening, was it?

Someone was actually knocking on the food truck service window?!

Maybe if she ignored them, they'd go away.

Isabella's fingers began typing again. She was fast. But now she tried to type as quietly as she could manage on a rather clickety-clackety keyboard.

BANG! BANG!

Great. Whoever it was must be *really* hungry!

———

Robin spied the top. Nearing it.

Good, because his upper arms were aching. Muscles burning.

He thought himself to be in good shape. But climbing ten thousand rungs on a ladder straight up seemed to argue with that opinion.

He only had maybe ten more yards until he hit the walkway above. A metal mesh that formed a narrow path around the outside of the electronics.

Robin finished the last bit of the climb and took in a deep

breath. Then, sticking out one awfully nice new boot, he stepped onto the walkway.

Solid.

Thank God!

It hadn't really worried him. He just had his doubts. And sometimes a person's imagination can get away from them if given half the chance.

In order to take another step—

He had to look down at the narrow walkway.

Through the metal grate that held him up.

Ugh. He would really rather not have looked through the holes. He needed to keep his eyes focused on things that were only a few feet away from him. That would do it. It would keep him from looking at anything farther away, like down below. The stuff that flipped his stomach!

A gust of wind picked up.

His arms windmilled!

Hands reaching—

Searching for something!

And he found it.

A thin handrail! Wobbly, but metal.

Phew.

Robin pushed his dinner down again. The quicker he got to work finding the point of the hacker's access, the quicker he could climb back down. He looked around.

There had to be about ten different closet-shaped metal boxes up there. All spread out around the inside of the square walkway. He'd have to go one by one and see what he could find. Who knew—maybe he'd get lucky and find the hack job on the first box.

Another ten feet above him were the active cell transmitters.

Up there, the RF waves were live and very active. Any closer to them and the radiation got intense pretty fast.

Robin inched his way closer to the first metal cabinet.

He reached out and twisted the handle.

Locked.

No problem. That was expected. And his team had made provisions for just this thing.

With the sounds of the city traffic down below and the wind whistling in his ear, Robin reached down under his coat and the collar of his shirt. Rummaging around, he lifted out a chain necklace—

And the security key attached to it.

The usable end of the key was cylindrical and had teeth splayed out all around it.

With one hand bracing himself on the metal cabinet, Robin leaned in ever so slightly, fitting the door lock with his key. A 3D print with the toughest PLA filament Anika could find.

This had to work.

There were plan B options on this operation.

But not for the key.

This was the weakest link. And the one that had concerned Robin from the beginning.

If their manufactured key broke inside the lock, that would be the end of things. Game over. Not only did they have time to print just one key, but then there would be the broken piece still lodged inside the lock. He had a pair of needle-nose pliers. But there was always the chance he wouldn't get anything to grip ahold of.

Robin gently turned the key. He didn't force it. He coaxed it to work. Willed it! And—

CLICK!

The lock unlatched. Perfectly!

The metal door on the tall, skinny cabinet swung open.

Robin carefully stepped back, letting the door open fully.

Okay, that went better than he had expected.

Robin smiled.

Maybe this job was going to be easier than he thought!

4

nika ducked into Chad's elevator just as the boy—
Pressed the button for the top floor.

Suddenly all business, Chad dropped his bag on the floor. He unzipped it. "Okay, I'm guessing we don't have long before security is on us."

"Aunt Whiney, excuse me?!"

"Huh? You like that?" Chad looked up with a smile. He continued to pull out one neatly folded article of clothing after another and arrange them on the floor.

"Um, no, as a matter of fact!" Anika huffed. "Don't you understand that your little performance down there is only going to draw *more* attention to us?!"

"Really? I thought it was rather well acted, personally," Chad said, slipping a long-sleeved button-down shirt over his Sponge Bob T-shirt. "You can't tell me you didn't start to care for my sweet aunt by the end, no?"

DING.

The elevator doors opened.

Anika smiled at a couple standing in the hallway—"Sorry, this is an emergency!"—and stabbed at the Close Door button.

Her smile disappeared as the doors slid shut again. "Where did you get all of that nonsense?!"

"Believe it or not, it was all improv," Chad said, stepping into a crisp, clean pair of black dress pants, tugging them up and over his shorts. "You probably think I should go into acting, don't you?"

"I—I—"

"That's alright. Trust me, I'll remember you when I get big in Hollywood. When I'm up there receiving my Oscar. I won't be like those highfalutin actors that snub their humble origins. I'll give you a shout-out, alright?"

Anika rolled her eyes.

"Aren't you gonna get dressed?!" Chad barked, hopping about trying to tug on a pair of wingtip shoes.

Anika reached up and grabbed the zipper just below her chin. *ZIPPPP!*

In one swift move, she peeled herself out of a pair of gray overalls. Underneath, she wore a stunning off-white dress and a simple but classy string of pearls. With another yank, she pulled her hair out of its tight bun. Her black, tightly curled hair filled out. "There, I win," Anika said with an edge to her voice.

"No fair!" Chad snapped as he twisted and turned an unknotted silk tie around his neck, his face getting red. "By the way, you have any idea how to actually tie one of these? I think I finally understand why guys think they're just a form of decorative noose."

"Here, give me that." Anika grabbed both ends of Chad's expensive tie. "Before you strangle yourself!" She had second thoughts about that. But it wasn't the time for more jokes. Anika had tied a man's tie before. She had helped her father several times. The most recent being at her grandmother's funeral.

Anika flipped one end over the other, wrapped it under. Then over.

She hadn't been this close to Chad in—

Anika didn't know when.

Annoying. Childish. Definitely not her type.

Where was she? Yes! She tucked the fat end of the tie down through the hole. Pulling gently against itself, it nicely formed a Half Windsor knot. A little fat, but good enough. She couldn't remember how to do the full version. No matter. It looked fine

Good enough to give them an edge over hotel security.

And that's all that mattered.

"Hey, you're pretty good at that," Chad said, staring at himself in the dim reflection of the rich, polished wood on the elevator wall. He tugged on a matching Irish tweed flat cap just as—

DING.

The elevator doors opened again. Top floor.

With one hand holding open the doors, Chad spun toward the control panel—

Then ran a finger over all the buttons.

Every light on the control panel glowed.

This had all been a part of the plan, but Anika still couldn't help but frown. Despite working for the good guys, tying up a perfectly good elevator for the next twenty minutes simply felt wrong!

Then out into the hallway strutted two incredibly dressed teens!

Unconcerned about the hallway camera.

The hotel floor was wide with expensive handmade Indian rugs running down the center of the hallway. The room doors were genuine wood, finished with a dark cherry polish. Between the doors, original framed artwork hung on the walls.

As they strode down the hallway, Chad slipped a small electronic adaptor from a pocket. He handed it over to Anika.

Using the USB-C connector, she plugged the adaptor into the bottom of her phone.

BEEP, BEEP, BEEP.

Her phone emitted a quiet sound, keeping a steady beat. On the screen, a proximity grid displayed an outgoing wave and its bounce-back return.

Chad approached a small alcove set back from the hallway. Turning to the side, he ducked inside it.

An ice machine. Chad looked around the machine. On top of it. Around the back.

There! An empty bucket.

They had gotten lucky someone left it there. Chad didn't delay. Grabbing it, he flipped open the lid on the ice maker and dug out a bucketful. Without looking, Chad held it out behind him.

Anika grabbed it.

Closing the lid on the ice maker, Chad glanced around the small recess.

An upper-class vending machine—if there was such a thing—offering samples of pricey perfumes and colognes. An espresso machine.

But Chad wasn't interested in any of that.

Instead, he turned his attention to a square hatch in the wall.

It was sizable. To the side of it hung a small sign, as though it were a piece of museum artwork. It read: LAUNDRY.

Without hesitating, Chad yanked the hatch open.

He peered down the dark, empty shaft. "Hello, down there!" His voice echoed off the metal walls that seemed to go on forever. Apparently satisfied, he tossed his empty backpack into the hole.

"Alright. Come on," Anika growled. "We've got a Stingray device to find somewhere across fourteen floors."

Chad closed the laundry door and reentered the main hallway.

BEEP, BEEP, BEEP.

Anika continued to pan her phone from side to side.

After a while, Chad broke the silence. "Would you ever slide down one of those?"

"Slide down one of *what*?"

"The laundry chute."

"No."

BEEP, BEEP.

"What if someone offered you a hundred bucks. Would you do it then?"

"No. I still wouldn't do it." Anika paused, looking up from her phone. "Just because someone offered me money doesn't mean I would immediately do something stupid. Do you have any idea how dangerous that would be?"

Chad nodded wholeheartedly.

"Or where one of those even goes?!" Anika whispered, keeping pace again, constantly tracking the signal on her phone.

BEEP, BEEP, BEEP.

"Yup, you're right," Chad said, trailing a bit behind. "That's why I'd do it for fifty bucks."

Anika stopped again. Her concentration broken.

"I don't know," Chad shrugged. "I might even do it for twenty."

5

sabella shut off the overhead light inside the food truck.

BANG! BANG!

Whoever it was clearly wasn't going away.

Trying her best to hide and cover the equipment, Isabella slid open the blackened side window.

She had her mouth already open.

Ready to chew out whatever annoying person thought that maybe, just maybe, the food truck was actually open for—

But it wasn't a single person.It was a long line of people.

All apparently waiting for the food truck to open!

"I'm—I'm sorry," Isabella said, changing her tone as best she could. "But we're—we're not open for business."

"What?!" the man in front of her practically yelled. He looked over his shoulder and yelled, "She said they aren't open!"

A collective groan rose up from the line.

Disappointment.

Frustration.

Where had all of these people come from?! Based on a quick glance down the line, they looked like an average cross section of city people. A guy wearing a hard hat and tool belt. A business-woman clutching her briefcase.

"Help me understand something," the man up front said with a manufactured smile. He wore a nice shirt with a cardigan tied loosely around his neck. He held up his phone and thrust it closer to Isabella. "If you are really closed, then why did you tweet about free cupcakes?!"

Isabella pulled back.

She had no idea what was going on in front of her.

The man continued. "And to the first one hundred visitors, no less. Huh?!"

Had Isabella fallen asleep at the computer—

And this was just a dream?

The cardigan man stabbed his finger at the screen. "Don't you see it? That's you—isn't it?!"

Sure enough, the image on his phone was of a food truck.

Colored the same as theirs.

It even had the same goofy name blazed over the side of it: THE SWEETEST THING.

Isabella pulled out her own phone and snapped a picture of his screen

She hadn't made such a tweet.

The truck wasn't even capable of making cupcakes anymore.

But Isabella had a greater problem on her hands.

An angry mob disappointed in losing out on their promised free dessert!

———

Robin spied it.

In the first cabinet.

An extra device. One that shouldn't be there!

It didn't take a cellphone technician to see that it didn't belong.

The device was an elongated cylinder that tapered, rounding off toward both ends. It stood on three fins and was pristine white: a mottled powder coating, from the look of it. The object was unlike anything else at the top of the tower, which had already collected what looked like a millennium's worth of dirt and grime.

Robin gently picked up the device, carefully examining it. There were no words on it. Just a thin ring of blue light running around it near the center. One cable extended from the device, plugging itself into the tower box's morass of wires and cables.

Robin gripped the cable extending from the cylinder and tugged on it.

POP!

It disconnected.

The blue glow from the device dimmed—

Until it was gone.

Beside the cable jack was a thin slit the size of an SD card.

Robin pressed in on it.

But nothing happened.

If there had been a data card inside, it should have popped out. If the thieves were stealing data, it only made sense that they would want to keep it. But then why wasn't there any card in—

Movement!

Robin saw it. Out of the corner of his eye.

In front of him. Through the narrow gap between phone boxes.

On the other side of the walkway.

It could have been a bird.

Sure, that was likely it.

He had seen the flock of blackbirds earlier on the climb up.

But that wasn't what he was seeing now.

No, this wasn't feathers.

This was a boot.

Or a fraction of one as it tried to hide itself behind another metal box.

Inky black. Laced. Combat style with steel toes.

Robin didn't move. He swallowed hard.

After what felt like a million ladder rungs, he was easily two hundred feet off the ground—

And *not* alone!

6

hile Chad worked at disconnecting the fire alarm on the stairwell door, Anika pressed her earpiece. "We've finished scanning the fourteenth floor. No joy."

Anika paused.

Awaiting a response she never got.

"I repeat: No joy on the fourteenth floor. Moving down one level."

Static.

Still no response.

Chad fastened the last of the alligator clips, spanning a connector. He pressed slowly on the emergency door's crash bar . . .

And nothing happened.

Good. He shot Anika a thumbs-up and struggled to squeeze through the door. It was a sweaty effort. Like playing the game Limbo, only sideways. After he made it through, Chad held the door open just enough, but not so far that it would break his thin connection.

Anika tucked the bucket of ice under her arm and, with her

ROB BADDORF

free hand, pressed her earpiece again. "Isabella, come in. Are you there?"

And in one graceful move, Anika slipped through the narrow opening with little to no effort.

"You gotta teach me how to do that," Chad whispered. "I'm more like a square peg in a round hole."

Anika raised one finger. "Robin, are you there?"

Silence.

"Hello, are we having problems with the comm?!"

She got nothing in return.

Anika and Chad made their way down the staircase. Bare concrete. Hollow sounds echoed off the wall. It was downright ugly compared to The St. Arcadia's fine interior.

Maybe the old adage "No news is good news" applied here.

Everything was probably just fine.

Running like clockwork.

Maybe all the concrete and metal in the building's structure was blocking her comm signal. No big deal.

Anika waited, watching as Chad worked on the thirteenth-floor fire alarm.

And a thought came to her. Just how dependent the team was on their communication devices. She felt like they simply could not do what they did without them. It was like driving a car without having access to GPS. The team would simply be lost without their electronic gear.

How did the FBI operate before all these modern-day gadgets? Back in the dark ages?!

There was no way it could have been any easier back then.

With his wire clips in place, Chad pressed on the crash bar.

No alarm.

"Alright, we're good to go. Ladies first," he whispered, making a gesture with his arm.

Isabella closed the window again, yanking the black curtain back in place across it.

She simply could not get tied up in all these people's problems!

She had a job to do.

And now she wasn't doing it!

Isabella wasn't responsible for those people outside. For their confusing her truck with someone else's. It happened!

Only, something continued to nag at her.

The tweet showed *her* truck.

In the exact location where it currently was.

How could that possibly happen?!

A mistake?

Or something more?

Even if it were nothing more than an elaborate prank, who would do that?

Isabella pulled up her photo of the man's phone. She eyed the hashtag and switched over to the X app. With a quick search, she found it: the original post. She shouldn't spend time on this. Not really. She simply wanted to check out a few things.

First the time/date stamp on the post.

Yup. Sure enough, whoever was behind this little joke had just posted it. Not twenty minutes ago.

But who? Why?

Isabella scanned the username.

It was short.

One of those odd names.

Zero Day.

Was this someone Isabella knew? A kid at school trying to get her attention? She thought about it, but no one came to mind.

Why would a random stranger play games with a food truck they knew nothing about?!

The name Zero Day triggered a few thoughts, but Isabella couldn't address them now.

She had a mission to help lead.

Not that anyone likely even knew she had gone off comms in the first place!

7

R obin had no weapon.

Nothing to threaten another invader with.

Or to use as defense!

Okay, he had to slow down. He had options here.

He just had to find them!

Maybe he should start climbing back down. That certainly sounded like a good idea. After all, Robin had disconnected the hacking device. He could clip it to his belt and simply get out of there.

That's what he really wanted to do!

But there was a problem with that plan.

If there had been an SD card in the device, he couldn't leave without it. Yeah, and how was that going to work itself out?! Was he just going to walk around to the other side and kindly ask whoever the person was up there with him if Robin could have it?!

Clearly, the other person knew Robin was there.

They must have gotten there first and now were hiding.

Was this the individual behind the hack?

Who else could it be?!

So many questions.

And no answers!

Robin felt stuck. He had to make a decision. He had to act!

But what to do?!

And that's when something helped him decide.

KR-THANGG!

He heard the sound first.

The terrible sound of metal colliding with metal!

But where had it come from?

Wait.

Down below?!

And then he felt it.

The tower suddenly shook violently!

Robin was not ready for that.

His arms went out in every which direction. Thrashing. Searching.

Hands ready to grab anything solid they could find!

In the process—

The hacking capsule slipped out from under his arm.

He watched it.

Tumble.

Twist through the air.

Whistling as it went.

As he himself would do next if he didn't get a good hold!

Robin gripped the metal cabinet box in front of him. The wires. Anything that felt like it would hold him.

Had something struck the cell tower?!

What was happening? An earthquake?!

Robin peered down once more. He just barely spied the white cylinder striking the ground. It burst into a thousand pieces. In every direction!

Well, hopefully Isabella didn't need that part anymore.

And it was then that Robin also noticed a tiny toy truck. Way down below. Backing up away from the base of the cell tower.

Was that what had struck the tower?! It had to be an accident. No one in their right mind would—

The truck lurched forward again!

This was no accident. Was the driver insane?!

He saw the vehicle ram squarely into the base of the communication tower.

Then he heard it again.

KR-THANGG!

He knew he only had seconds.

And wrapping his arms around a fistful of cables—

He gripped the metal cabinet even tighter!

As a terrible shock wave rose upward that—

Set the top of the tower dramatically swaying!

———

BEEP, BEEP, BEEP.

Tracking the source of this device was maddening. It almost looked like it moved!

Here one moment.

Gone the next.

It likely wasn't a large device. A Stingray machine was most commonly used by police forces. They used it to tap into conversations criminals were having and the data they were sending. Whoever had set this Stingray unit up clearly knew what they were doing.

Chad and Anika were down on the twelfth floor by now. And so far, no sign of security.

There were multiple hits on Anika's phone. But nothing was solid.

And guests inside the hotel were beginning to notice them.

A strange, well-dressed girl walking about, waving a phone in front of her.

And the unusually short boy that followed behind. Too old to be her son, too young to be a boyfriend.

BEEP! BEEP!

The signal intensified again.

It was here. It had to be!

Anika turned to door number 1214. Sure enough, the signal grew louder. Faster!

Clearing her throat, Anika knocked on the door.

Chad stood off to the side, his back pressed against the wall.

She didn't have the slightest idea whose room this was. Or whom they might be disturbing at this time of night. But they had a script preplanned. All Anika had to do was stick to it!

She stood in front of the door so that anyone inside looking out the peephole would not be startled. Tucking away her phone, Anika held the bucket of ice before her. The cover story was that she had simply gone to get ice and forgotten what room her parents were in. And she wondered if the occupants could call down to the front desk for help. It was as simple as that.

Anika practiced her lines.

Tried not to look nervous.

Only, she continued to stand there.

No answer.

She knocked again. Harder this time.

Waiting.

Was someone inside but just not answering?

This was the hard part.

Deciding when to go into a locked room, especially when you had no idea what or who was behind the door.

Surely she had waited long enough. "Hit it!"

Like he was on a hinge, Chad swung around.

Lockpicks in hand.

Already kneeling in front of the door, he worked on the lock.

Anika spun to face the hall.

She was now on guard duty.

Holding a bucket of ice.

Trying to look casual. Like they both belonged there.

Looking this way.

And that.

A housekeeping lady some distance down the hallway lifted a stack of fluffy white towels off her loaded cart of supplies. She appeared to be focused and hard at work. With her fresh supplies, the housekeeper reentered the distant room she was cleaning without even turning toward Anika and Chad. Good.

When—

DING.

It was a distant sound.

As the elevator doors opened.

And two rather tall, muscular gentlemen exited the elevator.

This was not good.

Especially the fact that both men were dressed identically.

In dark blue suits and with coiled earpieces.

Both held substantial walkie-talkies in their hands.

This definitely was *not* good!

8

An idea!

Isabella grabbed a sheet of clean paper out of the color printer mounted above her head.

If someone was going to play a joke on them—

Then she could play one too!

Grabbing a felt marker from a drawer, Isabella wrote:

FREE CUPCAKES GONE.

THANKS FOR YOUR SUPPORT!

COME BACK NEXT TIME!

SEER-RIP!

She tore off a piece of clear tape from the dispenser and applied it to the top edge of her sheet. Approaching the food truck's side window again, she could see fresh faces gathering already. All jockeying for position and forming a line.

Without hesitation, Isabella attached the sign to the window while mouthing the words "I'm sorry" to the folks outside.

Isabella dragged the black curtain back into place.

She could hear the groans of disappointment outside.

No matter.

The joke was over.

Isabella stepped over the box of metal vapor torches that still hadn't found a home and climbed back in front of her computer.

Donning her headset, she clicked her mouse and spoke. "Check, check. How's everyone doing?"

She didn't get an immediate answer.

"Hello? All quiet on the Western Front?"

————

Robin hunched down lower and held on for dear life!

It felt at least like a magnitude 8.0 earthquake!

Robin's AirPods shook themselves out of his ears. He watched as they—

K-TINK, TINK.

Bounced through the metal mesh walkway and tumbled back to Earth.

He had to get to the other side of the walkway. To the boots.

And the missing SD card!

But how could he when someone was ramming the tower?

Trying to kill them both!

Hand over hand, Robin clutched at anything solid that presented itself. As the intense vibrations diminished, he shuffled around the walkway. He had to go as fast as possible. And yet never let go!

Rounding the last corner, he peered around another set of metal cabinets to see—

A figure in all black.

Head to toe.

Only a thin slit revealed the person's eyes through their balaclava.

A pair of hazel eyes glared at him.

Filled with fear!

But sure enough—

There was something clutched in their hand!

KR-THANGG!

"Is that it?!" Robin yelled over the noise of bending and twisting metal. "Do you have the SD card?!"

He didn't get an answer.

Robin braced for it. For the next crippling shockwave about to arrive.

When it did!

The worst yet!

GROOWWRR!

The entire top section of the communication tower groaned—

Metal tearing away from metal—

And listed to one side!

Robin lost his footing.

Thrown forward.

His arms and hands flailing.

PING, PANG, PTANG!

Bolts in the underlying girders sheared off completely. Or exploded under the incredible strain!

And what Robin's hands found to grip was none other than—

The figure!

Up close, the eyes facing him were a mix of green and brown. Thick lashes.

And that was the last thing Robin remembered seeing clearly for quite a while.

Because the figure's black-gloved hand swung upward—

PSSSSSSSSS!

And sprayed liquid in Robin's face!

A burning liquid.

Absolute molten fire!

Pepper spray?!

Robin screamed, but thankfully he didn't let go. Or maybe he did. He couldn't remember. All he could remember for sure was going blind. And the figure grabbing onto him in return. For a brief instant, as if it were a wrestling match.

And at the most inopportune moment!

Just as the cell tower folded in on itself!

Then Robin felt one of the worst sensations he ever knew existed.

That of falling!

Of his stomach rising up inside his body cavity.

Of nothing solid below.

And of wind suddenly rushing past his ears.

Robin couldn't see the ground surging up to meet him.

But he did feel something.

An arm reaching across his chest.

Tugging on him.

No, on his backpack.

On the safety parachute cord!

FLOOPH!

It must have opened. Likely with only feet to spare!

The straps jerked him hard.

Like they would rip off both arms!

And the crushing weight of someone else clutching onto him.

Trying to maneuver and climb over him!

Why hadn't they landed yet?!

The hill. The cell tower had been on top of a rise, just on the edge of the city. Were they still going downward?!

"I need your help steering!" came a voice in his ear.

A female voice. Young.

Robin opened his eyes.

Or tried to!

They burned like nothing he had ever experienced before. Everything was blurry. Like trying to see through a fogged shower door.

"Here," the voice said again. "Pull on this when I tell you!"

Robin had no problem with obeying. Obeying *who* exactly wasn't even the issue right then. He honestly didn't care if this girl was with the bad guys or the next president of the United States. He merely wanted to live!

At best, Robin saw things as a blur.

"NOW!" she yelled straight in his ear, half-deafening him in the process.

Robin pulled.

What was he pulling?

The left steering toggle—yes, of course.

But what were they trying to avoid?!

All Robin could see was a large dark thing approaching.

He squinted away the tears.

For a moment, clarity returned.

As well as the side of an approaching building!

Robin yanked on the steering toggle as hard as he could.

The girl clutched onto Robin. Together, their bodies banked.

Becoming nearly horizontal.

And—

WHOOSH!

Skated just past the glass edge of the building!

What in the world?!

Robin had only hoped to survive the fall.

And now they were slaloming skyscrapers?

How were they supposed to survive this?!

9

"Chad," Anika whispered over the sound of the ice inside the bucket rattling. "You do understand we have company, yes?!"

The two security guards continued their march directly toward her.

"Don't rush me," Chad said, biting his tongue, focusing. "Beethoven never composed with a nagging coworker pushing him! True genius comes at its own pace. You can't rush that!"

The security guards turned to the side as they passed the housekeeper's cart.

"Well, you better kick your true genius into gear because—"

KR-CLICK!

Anika spun around.

Where was Chad?!

Like a magic trick, he had suddenly disappeared.

Just as the two security guards stopped in front of Anika.

She tried to smile.

To look like she knew exactly why she was holding a bucket of melting ice in front of her in the middle of a long hallway and doing nothing else but looking awkward.

"Are you alright, miss?" one guard asked.

"Um, sure," Anika managed to get out. Her throat felt dry and constricted. "I—I went to get, um, ice, you know. At the—the ice machine thingy." She stabbed a finger at the twelfth floor's identical alcove near the housekeeper's cart.

Hold on. Had she really just said "thingy"?!

Come on, she could do better than that!

"And then I forgot which room my parents are in," she said with a smile.

The two guards stood towering over her. Just staring at Anika.

With expressions on their faces like they thought she was dumb as a brick or—

Possibly up to no good.

The first guard narrowed his eyes. His walkie-talkie floated up to his mouth. "Um, dispatch. I need a room number for a—" He let go of the side button, his attention back on Anika. "What did you say your last name was?"

"Um. Didn't—Didn't I already tell you my last name?" Anika said in as normal a voice as possible. It likely came out little more than a whisper.

In unison, both guards shook their heads.

Did they just lean in closer to her?

Or was that only Anika's nerves?!

She didn't have a last name. Not one that would be registered in the hotel books. She could say whatever last name came to her mind, but if it wasn't in the guest registry then the gig would be up. The guards would grab her and drag her out of the—

"Oh, hey sis," a voice said from behind her. "There you are. What took you so long?"

Anika spun around.

Her face completely devoid of blood.

It was Chad.

Standing in the open doorway—

With one towel wrapped around his waist and another twisted over his wet hair like a turban. One arm casually propped up against the doorframe.

"You know Mom's not gonna be happy. Were you out looking for boys again?" Chad asked with a straight face. "Tsk, tsk."

The second guard cleared his throat while tugging up his belt. "Well, I'm glad you found your room. If you see a boy running around up here wearing a T-shirt and shorts acting obnoxious, call us, will you?"

"Will do, officer," Chad said with a wink, shooting a finger pistol at the security guard. Then Chad reached out and, grabbing the bucket, retreated into the room.

Anika couldn't quite follow Chad. Not yet.

She was still busy processing everything that had just happened!

———

Isabella checked the computer screen.

She hit the refresh button again, getting a clearer view on Anika and Chad's GPS tracker.

They were right where they were supposed to be.

Everything looked just fine with them.

But then she noticed it.

Robin's tracker.

Something was clearly buggy.

Isabella tapped the computer monitor as if somehow that might bring clarity.

It didn't.

From the looks of things, Robin was traveling halfway across the city.

And at quite a rapid speed.

But it was the altitude numbers that convinced her it wasn't correct.

It couldn't be! How—

KNOCK, KNOCK.

Not again!

But no. This time someone was knocking on the back set of double doors. Why there? Hadn't they seen the note on the server's window?!

She could just ignore them.

They would go away.

KNOCK, KNOCK.

Isabella jumped up from her seat. She was tired of this. If she needed to put a blasted note on every door, window, and exhaust pipe that they had NO cupcakes, then she would do that!

Only, when she pushed aside the blackout curtain by the back window—

It was no customer looking for a free handout.

The figure that stood before her looked more like a delivery person.

A woman wearing a food server's hat. The kind made of cheap paper and that looked like a boat.

Before the figure hovered a large white box with a shiny cellophane window across the top of it.

The woman looked to be struggling under the weight of it.

Isabella cracked open the door. "Yes, can I help you?"

"Oh, thank you!" the woman groaned, thrusting the box forward, wedging open the back door more. With just enough floor space, she plopped down the box. "Your shipment is here," she said gleefully as she turned around and grabbed another identical box.

"My shipment? I don't understand." Isabella frowned. "I didn't order anything."

A third box got stacked atop the other two before the delivery woman grabbed a clipboard, reviewing it. "Right here," she said, holding out the paperwork and tapping on it.

Isabella reluctantly reached out and took it.

Scanning through all the information.

What was this? She honestly hadn't ordered anything!

The delivery woman schlepped another white box on top of the growing tower.

What was inside all these boxes?!

As if on cue, the delivery woman dusted her hands and announced, "There you go. That should be the last of them. Bought and paid for: two hundred cupcakes!" She closed the back hatch on her car. "Don't eat 'em all at once. That'll give you quite a stomachache," she said with a smile and a simple salute as she climbed back into her car.

Bought and paid for? Two hundred??

Sure enough, when Isabella glanced down through the clear window on the top box—

There had to be dozens of brightly colored cupcakes inside.

Were the boxes honestly all filled with cupcakes? More and more of them?!

Dumbfounded, Isabella whispered to herself as the delivery car pulled away.

"But—but I didn't order any cupcakes."

10

Robin's eyes continued to water.

He could barely endure the burn.

Everything inside of him wanted to shut his eyes again.

To let his tears wash away the pepper spray. Along with everything else!

But he didn't dare close them again.

Oh, no!

And now he felt like he couldn't breathe.

Taking in a simple breath felt labored!

Was the girl behind him now? With an arm wrapped around his throat?!

"I can't—I can't breathe!" he tried to yell. But he couldn't do it. He couldn't get in enough air to force it back out again.

And what exactly was *that* ahead?

Were they actually approaching two buildings?

Or were the buildings coming toward them?!

HOOONNK!

The sound was loud, blaring!

And definitely not the sound that most buildings made.

Semitrucks!

Oh, dear Lord, help us!

Were they really going to thread the needle between two sixteen-wheelers?!

"A little less," the girl whispered close in his ear. "A little more, yes. Right there. Don't move it!"

Robin closed his eyes again.

Yes, because they were burning like a thousand suns!

But that wasn't the only reason.

Also because if he couldn't get in another breath—

He'd simply pass out!

WHOOOSHH!

The blast of air that washed over him as they squeezed between the two speeding trucks practically shoved air into his lungs for him! The forces were tremendous.

And then, just as quickly as they had appeared—

The trucks were gone.

"Now, you ready for this?!" the girl asked.

What?

There was more?!

"Get ready to run in place!" she screamed.

Robin ran.

With nothing underneath him, he ran like he had never run before!

And then it hit—

The ground!

Like a ton of bricks.

His knees begged to give up.

Only, Robin did his best to sprint—

While not seeing anything clearly.

Like the bright yellow block approaching.

A taxi?

That squealed around them.

As Robin and his passenger fell to the ground, dragged on concrete—more like sandpaper—the last twenty feet. Bouncing and spinning to a slow—

And eventual—

Stop.

Then that dreadful arm around his throat—

Suddenly disappeared.

"AHHHH!" Robin took in the deepest breath he could. Over and over again, gasping.

Rubbing his eyes.

Wiping away any pepper spray that he could.

He stumbled to his feet.

Standing before his attacker. His stowaway!

"Thanks for the ride!" the girl cheered. And with what looked like a wave, she took off running.

"Wait. No," Robin said, rubbing his eyes again. "Who are you?!"

But she was gone.

Did he dare take off after her?

Give chase?

Ha! Robin was doing plenty just standing up.

With eyes that barely worked.

And brush burns over his entire body!

———

Chad led Anika into the empty hotel room.

Such opulence!

Thick carpets. Crystal lamps. Sferra Giza 45 Luxe fitted bedsheets and covers proudly displaying their labels. An ornate

53

cherry wood writing desk.

"Do you want a mint?" Chad asked, slipping his clothing back over the shorts he wore underneath the towel.

"Mint? What mint?"

Chad gestured to the small squares of gold foil neatly placed on each pillow. "That one's yours—unless, of course, you don't want it."

Anika shook her head, pulling out her phone again.

BEEP, BEEP, BEEP!

The device was close.

Very close.

The sensor connected to her phone wasn't as sensitive as she would like. It didn't pinpoint the exact location of a Stingray device. It only got you close.

Close enough to hunt on your own.

But she was near it now.

Enough to stop using the phone?

Not quite.

The signal was most intense beside a closed door.

Anika hesitantly grabbed the doorknob, trying it.

Locked.

"It's behind here," she whispered.

"Doesn't that door connect with the next room?" Chad mused as he finished dressing and shoved another square of chocolate into his mouth. "It makes two rooms into one big suite?"

Anika nodded, stepping aside.

Slipping out his tools, Chad knelt before the door and got to work.

What would they find on the other side?

Should Anika be worried?

They hadn't made provisions for what would happen should the device be guarded. What then?

Or what if unsuspecting guests occupied the other room?

CLICK.

The door unlocked. Chad backed away like the entire thing was booby-trapped. Once clear, he gestured Anika over to it.

But she hesitated.

Wasn't there any way to tell what was on the other side of the door—

Before she opened it?

The short answer was no.

That was the answer she didn't like.

Anika reached out for the doorknob.

Her hand rested on the handle. As if she might somehow sense what awaited them. See it with her mind's eye.

She twisted it.

The door swung open on its own.

Anika held her breath.

The room looked unused. The bed sat neatly made. Untouched, from the look of things.

Except in the center of the large room sat another housekeeper's cart, stacked high with clean, folded bedsheets. There was a rack of tiny bottles. Shampoo. Lotions.

But it was what lay on the floor beside it—

Half hidden by the cart—

That caught Anika's attention.

A black combat boot.

Clearly connected to a leg.

Someone was on the other side—

Sitting on the floor!

11

Anika stepped forward.

Just as her phone made a flat tone.

BEEEEEE—

And a face peered out from around the back of the cart.

A face covered in an all-black balaclava. "No! Don't come any closer!" It was a male voice. "Leave! Get out now!" he said with desperation in his voice. "It's wired to blow!"

Who was this guy?

And why did he want them to leave?

About a million other questions raced through Anika's mind. But one stuck out more than any other.

What was wired to blow?!

The figure on the far side of the cart jumped to his feet. He tugged and yanked viciously on something, dragging the cart with him, until—

CRUNCH!

Whatever he was pulling off of it broke free!

In his hands was an electronic device. The size of an insulated lunch bag. With wires and antennae jutting out of it in every direction.

"You don't understand!" he yelled at them, heading for the room's main door. "It only has a fifteen-second timer!"

Anika froze.

It was too much information.

And all happening too fast.

Like drinking from a fire hose!

Time slowed.

And in the moment of paralysis, Anika noticed three things.

The first was that the figure dressed in all black ran out into the hallway. He was yelling about an explosion, trying to clear anyone from the area. Out of the corner of her eye,, Anika saw the figure grab the housekeeping lady and drag her out of the way.

The second was that Chad made a lunge for something. Something that quietly rested atop the room's bed pillows. Gold-foiled. She did *not* need to know any more about that.

It was the third bit of information that she focused on.

The small object that had just bounced on the carpet and now lay on its side.

Beside the abandoned housekeeping cart.

It had fallen out of the figure's device. When he turned and ran.

Anika knew it.

Knew its shape and form well.

An SD card.

But more to the point, she knew its importance!

And that's when she heard it.

TICK, TICK!

Slow. Deep. The housekeeper's cart counted off their seconds to live!

How much time had already expired?!

It didn't matter.

Anika sprang into action.

TICK, TICK!

She dove, tucking into a somersault.

And came out of it onto her two feet, with the SD card firmly in her hand.

"CHAD!"

Straining his fingertips Chad hesitated. The last mint was just out of reach.

"NOW!"

She would not say more.

TICK!

Because time was gone!

Sprinting out into the hallway, Anika glanced left, right. All clear.

But how strong would the explosion be?

There was no way to know.

Anika did the unthinkable.

Dodging past the ice machine, she yanked open the square metal door, identical to the one they had seen on the fourteenth floor.

Chad dove first. "WHEEE!"

If the fall didn't kill Chad—

She promised herself she would!

TICK!

Anika didn't hesitate. And just as she leaned forward into the dark, nasty laundry chute—

KR-BLAMMMM!!!

12

obin limped into the empty grocery store.

The group's headquarters.

As he walked, he continued to tilt his head back, pouring his water bottle over his eyes.

"Want a cupcake?" a voice said beside him.

It sounded like Isabella.

"We've got chocolate or vanilla," she continued, putting one in his hand. "And just about every color icing imaginable."

"Do you have any with sprinkles?" Chad asked.

Where was he?

Robin blinked a few times and found which one of the moving blobs was Chad. His eyes were getting better now. After another hour of rinsing, that should do it. At least, that's what he found on Google. He hoped he'd read the blurry information correctly.

Robin felt for one of the chairs around the center desk. Finding one, he plopped himself down into it, too exhausted to even eat the cupcake.

"Are we gonna give reports, Chief?" Anika asked.

Robin found the energy to nod.

"Alright, Chad and I will go first," Anika said. "The long and short of it is that we found the Stingray. Unfortunately, we lost it to some guy."

"Some guy?" Isabella asked. "Any more useful descriptors? Dark hair? Tattoos?"

"Muf donna mee," Chad said with his mouth completely stuffed.

"Um, let me interpret that for you," Anika said. "We couldn't see?"

Chad nodded.

"That's because whoever this guy was, he wore a tight black outfit, from head to toe. All we could see were his—"

"Eyes?" Robin interrupted, rubbing his own. "Did the guy wear black combat boots too?"

"Yeah, how did you know?"

"Because I stumbled onto his other half somewhere—I don't know—about six hundred feet in the air," Robin said, licking a fingerful of icing from his cupcake. "Female. Dressed exactly the same. We got to know each other much better on the way down."

"Really?" Isabella said, raising an eyebrow.

"Hey, don't read into that," Robin added quickly. "The only problem is that I lost the SD card in the process. All the data they were collecting—it's gone. She likely has it."

"Not anymore," Anika said, stepping forward. She presented an SD card between her fingers. "I got the back-up data files from off the Stingray itself."

"Wait a minute. Hold up." Chad wiped his mouth with a sleeve. "Let me get this straight. We had two bad guys dressed in all black, stealing data from cell phones, right?"

"Yeah, it's called a Stingray device," Isabella said, pulling up a few images on the computer of the device they had seen earlier. "You guys had one yourself, back when you hired me. Likely didn't know a whole lot about it, but the police like to use them. It functions much like a cell tower, only you can drive it around. Hide it in a police vehicle—"

"Or in a housekeeper's cart," Anika added.

"Precisely," Isabella said. "The only remaining question is, what do they want with the data they stole?"

A silence settled over the group as the thought sank in.

"That's not the only question," Robin said finally. "I don't think the two figures in black were the bad guys."

Isabella peeled the paper off a bright pink cupcake. "Why do you say that?"

"Because someone just so happened to ram the cell tower the two of us were on. I don't think they wanted us to get the data," Robin said, adjusting his seat. "Whoever was driving the utility truck into the cell tower didn't care if we lived or died. I'm wondering if we have more than one group of people we're dealing with."

"More than one?" Anika asked. "Like who? Why?"

Robin shook his head.

He took a bite of his cupcake.

The sugar rushed into his system, giving him a burst of energy.

"By the way," Chad said, beginning on his fifth cupcake, "if you ever get the chance, you really should try riding down the laundry chute at a hotel."

"No, you should *not*!" Anika growled. "Don't listen to him." She pointed at her accomplice. "Don't do it for ten or fifty dollars. Don't even do it for a hundred dollars!" Anika's face softened. "But if there is an explosion of that magnitude, I suppose then it isn't so bad of an escape route. I mean, when you consider the alternatives, of course."

"Of course," Robin said with a grin.

Isabella pushed her chair away from the computer. "There might be more than one group involved with the cell tower and inside the hotel, but that still doesn't deal with the issue of the pranksters. Someone posted a photo of our new command center —the food truck—and sent hundreds of people to it."

"Really? Why?" Chad asked.

"For free cupcakes."

"Ha, that's funny!"

"It might have started off that way," Isabella said. "But it quickly became a nuisance. I couldn't get my work done. I was off comms more than I was on them. That's not good. Then of course, to finish the joke, they sent me these cupcakes to give away. The ones that we didn't have because we're not a real food truck."

That gave Robin pause.

There was more at play here than they were understanding. More going on behind the scenes than he could fully comprehend.

Yet!

"We should probably paint the truck," he offered. "Something generic, so that no one believes it's actually a functioning food truck selling anything."

Nods rippled through the group.

"But I've had enough for one night," Robin said, standing up.

Or tried to!

Every muscle in his body felt stiff.

Sore.

"I'm going to bed!"

13

obin missed his alarm.

He slept right through it and didn't wake until closer to lunchtime.

Thankfully, it was a Saturday. Otherwise he would have had to come up with some excuse for missing school.

In the bathroom, he examined his eyes in the mirror. A little red and puffy but nothing worse. Had his dad ever been hit with pepper spray on the job?

As far as Robin could tell, he could see just fine now.

Robin showered, got dressed.

Only, as he tied his sneakers, he paused.

Maybe he was looking at last night's girl all wrong. If she wasn't part of the bad guys ramming the tower, then she likely hadn't put the hack device in place either.

But why *was* she there?

It was very unlikely she just happened to be up urban exploring the top of the city's tallest cell tower, right then. Somehow she had gotten intel on what was happening.

But how?

And from where?

And why would she have wanted the SD card for herself?

Was she just another thief trying to steal from the original thieves?

Robin knotted his shoes.

And grabbed his skateboard.

"I'm going out for a ride, Mom!" he yelled before hitting the back door of his house.

———

Isabella sat before the laptop on the desk in her room.

It chugged away. Fields of data streaming up the screen only to be replaced by more.

She had programmed it before going to bed. A sorting algorithm. Something to make sense of the terabytes of data on the SD card. In just a few hours, the scammers had collected more data than an army of humans could sift through in their entire lifetime.

Isabella just sat there watching her program run. She had an armful of clothing she had picked up off the floor. The clothes were supposed to be finding their way back to her drawers. But somehow watching all that data-crunching was like sitting before a campfire. Mesmerizing. Just seeing the machine do that much processing was impressive. The absolute beauty of technology!

But what were the data thieves after?

Generic information they could take advantage of? Passwords? Bank accounts?

Or something more specific?

Isabella wasn't against sorting the data herself. But the program was so much more efficient.

How did humanity ever survive before computers?!

———

Anika skateboarded on the outskirts of her town. She often did this on Saturday mornings. With the farmers market set up for one day only, it was a lovely place to grab brunch. Look at the cut flowers.

With an orange juice in one hand, she skated through a crowded parking lot.

It made for an interesting obstacle course.

The key thing about it was to keep an eye out for the little white lights.

Reverse lights.

Oftentimes when someone was backing their car out of a spot, they wouldn't be looking for pedestrians. Especially ones on top of a skateboard.

Today, though, she was having a hard time staying alert. Who was the male figure last night? The one dressed in all black.

And more importantly, why had he warned Anika and Chad about the explosive? For some reason, it had looked like he cared.

If he had been the one to plant the Stingray in the cart in the first place and was simply there to retrieve it, why warn them? And why was he struggling to get the box of electronics out if he had arranged it there in the first place?

Taking a swig of her orange juice, Anika kicked against the ground. Her board shot forward with a new burst of speed.

Anika felt like she had a handful of puzzle pieces.

But none of them fit together.

And she couldn't see the box top to know if they were part of the same puzzle or not.

It was almost as if the figure in black wasn't the perpetrator.

Could he have been like the Sneaky Inc. team?

After the same things they were?!

———

Isabella grabbed a few more articles of clothing off her floor. A sock with no immediate match. A T-shirt. Underwear.

She moved toward her laundry hamper when a new thought struck her.

Sending two hundred cupcakes to a nonworking food truck must have cost someone a lot of money. There was no way that much flour and sugar came cheap.

But who would spend that kind of cash for nothing more than a joke?

And could the money somehow be traced?

The armful of clothing fell back onto the floor.

Abandoned once more.

Isabella pulled her rolling chair up to the desk again. Her fingers flying over the keyboard.

It wasn't likely she could trace it if someone had paid the bill in cash. It would only work if the pranksters used a credit card. That or an online service to transfer the money.

First things first.

Who made the cupcakes?

Isabella remembered seeing it: the sticker and logo on the side of the boxes. Only, she couldn't remember the name of the bakery.

She pulled up Google Maps and typed in "cupcakes."

About a dozen little red pins dropped onto the map displaying her local area.

She began flipping through the different options until—

That was it!

McKinley Bakery.

Isabella jumped up from her seat and ran out her bedroom door.

Only to duck back inside and grab her board!

14

"Thanks for meeting me," Robin said as Chad pulled up. His friend kicked up his skateboard and grabbed it out of the air.

Then Chad looked up at the building before them.

Department of Motor Vehicles.

"You really wanted to come to this place on a Saturday morning?" Chad asked as they pushed their way through the front doors. "Isn't it a madhouse this time of week?"

"When isn't it?" Robin said with a wry grin.

"Well, you've got a point there." Chad nodded. "So, why are we here? You just got your driver's license. Did you forget to sign up for the organ donor sticker?"

"Um, that's not a bad idea," Robin said, grabbing a paper ticket with a number on it from the dispenser. "But no. I already did that."

The two wandered into the overcrowded middle area.

It looked like a giant cafeteria of sorts.

One section had waiting areas around small tables where some individuals did work. Or watched videos on their phones.

Other sections were filled with rows of seats.

Most of them overflowed with a mix of humanity.

Robin looked at the number on his slip. No. 422.

A voice came over the loudspeaker. "Now serving number one hundred and twenty-seven."

Robin and Chad slumped into a pair of open seats. Hard plastic, sculpted to something other than the human body. They had some time to kill.

"So, if we're not here about your license, then what?"

"Did you know," Robin leaned in and whispered, "that most street-view camera footage is part of the public record?"

"I did not know that," Chad said without even a trace of whispering. "Nor do I immediately understand why I would begin to care about something like that."

"I want to see if I can find footage from last night. Footage that involved the truck down below me."

"You mean, the one that wasn't so gifted at parallel parking and brought the entire cell tower down?"

"Yes, that one. And keep your voice down, will ya?" Robin looked around to see if anyone was listening. "I figure maybe if we get lucky, we could snag a license plate off it. Trace the vehicle back to an owner."

"Ohhh, I see," Chad finally whispered. "Very clever." He nodded. "I likey!"

———

Following the GPS on her phone, Isabella skated up to the front door of McKinley Bakery. She had never been there before. And as far as she could remember, she had never even driven past the place.

She pulled open the front door.

DINGLE, DING.

It triggered a pleasant little bell.

A voice called out from behind the counter. "Welcome to McKinley. It's the yeast we can do!"

Seriously? They greeted everyone who came into the place with baking puns?

But the store had a pleasant look to it. With bright yellow walls and crisp white trim, the place felt quaint. Cozy, somehow.

And the smell—

It was to die for!

Bread, doughnuts, and every kind of confectionary delight.

It smelled like a slice of heaven!

"Fancy meeting you here," a voice beside Isabella said.

Isabella spun around to see—

Anika!

"I got to thinking last night," Anika said, sitting at a nearby table. A wide cup of something dark and yummy-looking sat in front of her. "That maybe we could find out who was so kind as to gift the group so many cupcakes."

"I had the same idea," Isabella said, sitting across from her friend. "Did you already ask them?"

"I just did."

"And?! Did they remember what the person looked like?"

Anika shook her head. "They weren't about to forget an order for two hundred cupcakes. They don't get those kinds of orders very often. More like for weddings or a large business celebration."

"But they don't remember who put in the order?"

"It wasn't a walk-in, unfortunately," Anika said, sipping from her hot drink. "It was online."

"Ugh. It figures." Isabella slumped back into her chair. "So, I guess that's a dead end."

"Not entirely. First of all, you'll never guess when the bakery set up their ability to take online orders."

"No, when?"

"Yesterday."

"Seriously?! And this purchase of two hundred cupcakes was their first order?"

Anika nodded. "Becky, the lady behind the counter, was very friendly. She told me they've been wrestling for months with making the online ordering part of their website work. None of them are very techy. Then, just out of the blue, it starts working."

The smile on Isabella's face waned.

None of this sounded right.

Things in the land of HTML and Javascript rarely "just" started working. Especially not on their own.

Isabella leaned forward again. "She didn't say anything about the payment, did she?"

Anika shook her head. "She didn't. I'm assuming that part of things was okay. Real money from somewhere. But Becky did ask if we enjoyed them."

"Oh, I hope you told her they were delicious!"

"I did. I told her we liked them *so* much we wanted to thank her and the person who sent them."

Isabella's eyebrows rose.

Anika pushed a little slip of paper toward Isabella.

On it was a name.

Not a normal English name like Bobby or Annette.

A shiver of ice ran down Isabella's spine.

For the simple words on the paper were likely merely the user-name behind the generous gift.

Zero Day!

15

sabella sat in a contemplative silence in the group's somewhat dismal headquarters. Using her fingers, she rotated a rubber band between them to keep herself busy. Atop the one and only desk in the center of the expanse, her laptop continued to process information beside her. An oscillating fan swayed back and forth over it.

Anika sat not far away, twisting some mythical animal out of a handful of coffee stirrers.

The empty grocery store had its own ecosystem.

A leak in the far corner fed a patch of tall grass growing inside the building.

A barely perceptible cloud of ghostly white hovered just below the ceiling lights.

Robin and Chad finally entered from the back.

"Hey, where're the cupcakes?" Chad asked. "I'm hungry. And growing boys need their cupcakes."

"Ugh," Anika groaned. "I stuck 'em in the fridge." She pointed to the official Sneaky Inc. break fridge: a reworked machine she had pulled from the neighbor's trash and fixed. "I mean, they were tasty and all, but I'd be happy not to see another cupcake for the rest of this year."

"Really?" Chad said, yanking out several cupcakes. With one in each hand, he had to balance the third and fourth on his forearm. "I don't think I'll ever get tired of these!"

"Good, 'cause you can have the rest of them, Chad." Robin marched toward the central desk. "All one hundred and seventy-eight of them!"

"What if I have a bake sale?" Chad asked. "Can my department have all the money I earn from selling them?"

"Knock yourself out," Robin said, grabbing a chair. He spun it around backward and sat in it, turning his attention to the girls. "What did you find?"

Anika motioned for the computer expert to start.

"Alright," Isabella said. Her rubber band stopped rotating. "I've had my laptop running through this data all night long. Go ahead and feel it. It's toasty-hot from processing that crazy amount of information. And it still isn't done."

"Have you gotten any hits so far?" Robin asked. "Anything useful?"

Isabella sighed.

She wasn't sure where to even start with explaining it all.

"Alright, I started first with tracking names. From emails, transcripts, you name it. I figured maybe I could find a commonality with what I'm calling the 'high-end users.'"

"What's that mean?" Chad asked, spitting cake.

"A high-end user is either a name that continues to appear or one connected with any of the local Fortune 500 companies. I figured anyone rich and powerful might be a good target that the data hackers were after. You know, a quick grab at money. Or blackmail."

"And did you find any?" Robin asked.

"No." Isabella went back to working the rubber band between her fingers. "And that seemed surprising to me. So, if it wasn't that kind of low-hanging fruit, I figured next on the list might be financial passwords."

"Like PIN numbers on debit cards?" Anika asked.

"Yes, exactly like that. But I started bigger than an individual's bank accounts. I started with government organizations, moving down to corporate accounts. Still there was next to nothing in there. At least, nothing all that useful if you were going after money as your main objective." Isabella's rubber band kicked into motion again. High gear. Rotating at twice the speed as before. "I found a few people's bank accounts that are vulnerable. But nobody with any money worth talking about. If the hackers were after cash, it would be easier to go mug someone in a back alley."

Robin adjusted his chair. "Then they must be after something else."

"Hey, I'm all ears if you have an idea of what that might be," Isabella said. "But you wanna know what I *did* find?"

The others nodded, leaning in a little.

"I had my program search for repeated phrases." Isabella turned her attention to her screen. "The phrase 'Buy milk' was number one. 'Eggs' was number two. Anyone want to guess what the third most popular phrase was across all emails, phone calls, text messages, and the like?"

"'What's new on Netflix?'" Chad offered.

"No, but you're close," Isabella said. "'How's your day going?' and 'What's for dinner?' were tied for third place."

The group laughed.

"'What's for dinner?'" Anika joked. "Seriously? Then it's probably something that uses milk and eggs. Like pancakes!"

The group laughed even more.

It was funny and all.

But they weren't making progress with any of the puzzle pieces.

And that felt discouraging to Isabella.

The answer was there. In front of all their eyes.

Only, she couldn't see it.

Lost in an absolute sea of data!

16

obin got up. He felt antsy. He needed to move again.

His head lifted toward the ceiling.

This was his standard way of thinking. Of getting more oxygen to the brain.

He didn't care about the details of it.

It just seemed to work.

Robin began pacing. Up and down the long aisles for shelves that were no longer there. Only the rusty markings on the flooring hinted at their former locations. He knew the group could make headway with last night's incident. With all the questions before them. They simply needed a lucky break. A foot in the door.

Wisdom!

And straight from the source too!

Yes, that's what they really needed.

A way to see through the confusion and darkness.

Order from chaos!

"Lord Jesus," he mouthed the words. "Will you give us wisdom? Knowledge? And without finding fault in us. Especially in me."

His pacing stopped. Robin stared up at one of the ceiling lights. The ones Anika had rewired to the utility pole and got working when they moved into the abandoned grocery store.

One of them blinked.

With the gentle, damp haze up by the ceiling, the light produced soft rays. The beams stretching out from it.

Robin spun around. "Isabella, on your computer, look for the term *pepper spray*. Did your program find any reference to that phrase specifically?"

With a burst of fresh energy, Isabella spun around in her seat and typed.

A new search window appeared on the second monitor.

In spurts, a progress bar filled from zero to one hundred percent.

ZERO RESULTS.

"No," Isabella said. Her shoulders slumped. "Nothing."

Robin hunched over Isabella's shoulder, staring at the screen. "Try the words *tear gas*."

ZERO RESULTS.

Hmm. He thought for sure that would stir up something.

"*Tear gas* certainly is an unusual thing," Isabella said, looking up at Robin. "And clearly not a commonly conveyed phrase."

That got Robin thinking again.

He paced.

"It is unusual," Robin said, tapping his chin. "Can you give me a list of other unusual words?"

"Oh, I guess. I'd have to run it against a frequency dictionary first," Isabella said as she began pulling up one new window after another. "You're gonna get a lot of hits, you understand?"

Robin pressed in again, watching Isabella do her thing.

He could smell her perfume, or whatever it was.

He blinked, trying to focus on business. On the words on the screen!

"Then give me the unusual ones that were at least spoken, written, or sent more than once. "

A large database of results filled.

It was crazy just how big it was. In the thousands.

Random words like *peanut butter, fraction, Panama, carpet, license.*

But slowly the database whittled itself down.

Until a rather odd collection remained:

Demonstration

Crowe

Wavelike

Atoll

Pound cake

Electromagnetic oscillation

Champ

HIJENKS (Which was odd because they misspelled it—and more than once?!)

HPM

"What's that?" Robin pointed.

"HPM?" Chad said, inching forward. He peeled off the icing on a cupcake and, dangling it above his mouth, ate it plain. "It sounds like an acronym."

Isabella googled it.

The list looked long.

"Oh, wow. Okay," she said, clearing her throat. "It could be health policy and management, health policy monitor, high-pressure melamine—whatever that is!—or about a million more options. High-pressure mercury, high-powered microwave, historical photographs of mining . . ."

Robin leaned away from the screen.

This wasn't helping.

Nothing was.

It all seemed like chaos!

Was he waiting on God? Or was his team simply rushing ahead, trying to figure it all out on their own?

He honestly had no idea.

It all sorta felt the same.

"Forgive me, Lord, when I rush ahead of you," Robin prayed under his breath. "Help me to wait on you and your timing. Let me lean not on my own understanding."

Robin tapped his foot.

He was waiting, wasn't he?! It sure felt like it!

Isabella leaned away from the keyboard, looking stymied.

"Didn't you guys go to the DMV this morning?" Anika asked, breaking the silence. "How did that go?"

Robin wouldn't answer. He shrugged and motioned to Chad.

Chad provided a thumb drive to Isabella, who plugged it in.

The two girls watched.

As several videos opened simultaneously and played.

It was video all right.

But it looked more like a slideshow.

An image here.

Then something like two seconds later came another image.

It wasn't smooth motion.

"Go ahead," Robin grumbled. "Zoom in on the truck's license plate."

Isabella did.

There were only three frames where it was visible.

And even then, she couldn't make out any numbers or letters.

"They have a license plate blocker installed over it," Chad

said, peeling another cupcake. How many was that already? Where was the boy shoving them? Down a hollow leg?!

"It flocks the cameras from fetting a good fiew," he muttered with his mouth full. Chocolate crumbles dribbled down his shirt.

"Uh-huh," Isabella said, wrinkling her face at him. "I think we get the point. Between the tinted windows and the license plate blocker, the footage gives us nothing."

17

Robin tooled around on his skateboard, lost in thought. He was out behind the grocery store circling their half-pipe. With the occasional kick, he would roll forward. And then he waited. Waited until his board moved slowly . . .

Slower . . .

To the inevitable and agonizing stop!

Then, at the speed of a snail—

His foot would stretch out again.

And there would be another kick against the ground.

That would shoot him forward. A new burst of speed and movement!

Only through entropy and friction—

To slow again.

Slower . . .

And stop.

Robin wasn't exactly happy about waiting on the Lord.

The FBI had hired Robin and his whole team to do a job. And as far as he knew, he thought the Lord had wanted him to do it too.

But now they *weren't* doing it.

They were doing what felt like a whole bunch of nothing.

Nothing moving toward nowhere.

And fast!

———

The entire Sneaky Inc. crew came back after dinner for a party.

A painting party!

Isabella had drummed the whole thing up.

She claimed it was a chance to get the group smiling again. Maybe even laughing, if that was still possible.

And besides, the food truck needed some attention.

This wasn't supposed to be "work." Rather, a time to put on some music in the late-day sun and play again.

Anika had even ordered food and drinks for everyone. Hoagies to split. Turkey and bacon. An Italian with everything on it (including hot peppers, which were the best!). And chicken parmesan.

Robin looked up at the long pole in his hand. At the top end sat what looked like a long, fuzzy toilet paper roll.

A paint roller.

Each of his friends had a similar paint roller. Some longer than others. A base coat of white was beginning to cover up the faded colors of the previous owner.

Chad was the first to attack the big words on the side of the truck: THE SWEETEST THING.

At first, he slashed a broad stroke of goopy white paint over the middle, making it read: THE THING. He even made an argument to keep it that way, but was quickly outvoted.

Anika put on some old-time music by someone named Louis

Armstrong. It might have been old, but it sure got everyone tapping their feet.

It wasn't half-bad for a painting party!

Robin rolled the first coat over the pale pink back door.

A ghostly white streak followed closely behind his roller. Somehow it felt satisfying to cover over the things of old.

Like new wine for a new wineskin.

It was fun!

Where had it gone, exactly?

That sense of play.

Had they lost it completely? What they were doing these days had been more toilsome and less enjoyable. After putting Marlin Ledger away forever, their work became mostly wiretaps again. Swiping data files out of old filing cabinets buried in the basements of corporate buildings.

Sure, they were still getting paid, but there was something missing.

Maybe something on the edge of risk and play.

And now that his jump off the cell tower was over and his brush burns were nicely scabbing, Robin fondly reflected on it.

Okay, not fondly! That would be too strong of a word.

And no, he definitely would not call it fun. Not exactly.

But there had been something thrilling about it.

It felt like they had a real mission on their hands again.

A real mission, perhaps. But one that wasn't making any progress.

And that's when it hit him—

Right in the middle of pushing his roller through the tray of paint. As a slosh of thick white paint rolled out the back of the tray.

"Waves!" Robin blurted.

Apparently his outburst interrupted another of Chad's dumb jokes.

Everyone paused and turned toward him.

Robin continued to stare down at the tray.

"Did you say 'waves'?" Anika asked.

Robin pointed and then shoved his roller through the tray again.

Sure enough, it created a wave in the paint.

Which sloshed over the far edge—

And knocked over someone's half-empty Mountain Dew bottle.

"Hey!" Chad yelled. "I wasn't finished with that. And you're wasting paint. What's the deal?"

Robin looked up at his friends.

A crooked smile growing across his face.

18

sabella felt concerned.

Robin still hadn't been tested for a possible concussion after his parachuting incident.

That wasn't such a farfetched possibility, now was it?

He had been a bit more spaced out than usual.

Staring at things.

Lost somewhere inside of himself.

But Robin looked excited. "Do you remember some of the less common words we discovered throughout all the cell data?!"

He got a few nods, but mostly he got looks like maybe the group thought he had just lost his sanity.

"*Wavelike* was one of them. Remember that?!" Robin said, dropping his painting pole outside onto the asphalt. "And *electromagnetic oscillation*—that's wavelike, isn't it?" He didn't wait for an answer. "And *HPM*. Wasn't that an acronym for high-powered micro*waves*?!"

"I don't know," Anika whispered, offering a simple shrug.

"I think you're pushing it, Robin," Chad said before draining the last of his soda. "Grasping for straws? That last one has more to do with heating leftover dinner, doesn't it?"

Isabella hesitated. "Yeah, I'm not so sure either. It does feel like a bit of a stretch." She offered a shrug. "Sorry."

Seeing all this opposition only made Robin laugh.

"I see it. I mean, I *really* see it!" he blurted. "Like the Holy Spirit highlighted it for me. Right in front of my eyes! And now that I've seen it—" he yelled, abandoning his painting supplies and sprinting for the back of the store—"I can't unsee it!"

Robin slipped through the chain on the back door—

And was inside. Gone!

Isabella turned to the others.

No one had moved. Not even an inch.

In turn, they each quietly set down their own painting supplies. Anika shut off the bluetooth speaker and disconnected her phone.

So much for a party.

The atmosphere among the group now felt heavy.

Like rain on a parade.

Isabella wanted to give Robin the benefit of the doubt. She did. But he was grasping at straws. For the thinnest semblance of meaning that simply didn't exist.

They had all looked at the data.

Why didn't anything show up for them?

For her?!

If there really was meaning hidden in that chaos, did that mean God no longer spoke to her. Loved her?!

She hadn't read her Bible recently. Maybe this was punishment.

Or what about all the other junk in her life?

Her sin?

The group marched slowly back to the grocery store's rear entrance.

Clearly, Isabella had loads more work to do—

Just to make things right between her and God!

————

Robin grabbed the computer mouse and wiggled it.

The three monitors blinked on, awakening.

He was busy searching the Internet for the definition of electromagnetic oscillation.

He could hear his friends approach.

But he was too busy reading!

"Listen to this," Robin said. "Electronic oscillation is a repeating cyclical variation in voltage or current in an electrical circuit, resulting in a periodic *waveform*."

"Okay, fine," Chad said, his arms on his hips. "I'll give you the very rare chance that a few of those words all have to do with waves. But I wanna know how *fruitcake* fits into that, huh?!"

Robin opened his mouth—

But he didn't have an answer.

"Unless, of course, there was a fascinating conversation about someone surfing on a wave of fruitcake. That would be interesting, mind you," Chad said, licking his lips. "Especially if they use my grandma's recipe."

"And what about *hijinks*?" Anika asked. "Is that about having a fun time? What we were just doing?! How does that have anything to do with waves?"

"Alright, yes," Robin said, scrunching his forehead. "Some of these words or phrases may not fit as well as others do. But what do you think are the chances that at least three of them do?!"

There was a lot of headshaking.

"So what?" Chad asked. "Let's say you're right. What does the crashing of waves have to do with anything anyway?!"

Holding his chin, staring at the data before him, Robin tapped a finger against his cheek.

He knew it was there. Close. But he wasn't seeing the connections as well now.

Then it was Isabella's turn to gasp!

"Oh, wow!" she whispered, sipping from her bottle of iced tea. "Oh, WOW! Now *I* see it!" she blurted, laughing and choking on her drink at the same time.

"Are you alright?" Anika asked, concerned. She slipped her arm around the girl.

Isabella continued to cough. Clearly having something go down the wrong pipe.

"Do you need CPR?!" Chad yelled. "'Cause I know it, but I really don't like the mouth-to-mouth part," he said, squirming. With his hands up, he backed away. "You know what? I'll let Robin do it!"

"I'm fine," Isabella managed to get out. She was still hunched over. "I'm good."

"'Cause, if you ever notice the way Robin looks at you," Chad went on, without even a modicum of hesitancy, "he'd be *glad* to do it!"

19

obin felt his face turn red.

He would punch Chad. Oh, he most certainly would! It was all a matter of *when* was the right time? And *how hard* could he punch the jerk?!

Isabella looked up.

Her face was red too.

Was that from nearly choking to death?

Or something else?

She seemed to regain her composure quickly enough. At least she was breathing normally. Phew.

"I'll ignore that last little interchange," Isabella coughed. "What I suddenly remembered was one of the business names." She plopped herself in front of the computer again and, using a combination of the mouse and keyboard, dug through the data. "To be honest, I didn't give it much thought. You see that?" She pointed at the screen.

Bodies leaned forward.

Robin squinted. "Stanford Wave Laboratory?"

"Hold up," Chad chuckled, picking at a patch of white paint on his arm. "Can someone explain this to me? What kind of waves are we talking about here? This isn't the kind you give your mom when you're heading out the door for school, is it?"

That got a few laughs.

"Correct me if I'm wrong," Anika said. "But these phrases are talking about electromagnetic waves. For example, colors. Like red or purple. They both travel through the air as a wave. And each of them has a unique wavelength different from any other. We learned about this in class, Chad. You don't remember?"

"Um, a little."

"When you put white light through a prism, it splits it back into all the separate wavelengths."

Chad nodded. "Okay, so we're dealing with people messing around with the rainbow?"

Isabella pulled up an online graphic. "Colors and the visible spectrum are only a small part of the full electromagnetic wavelength. The others are all invisible to the human eye. Like radio, infrared, or even X-ray. They're all part of the same continuum."

"With each having its own wavelength," Anika added. "Some bigger. Some smaller."

With his brow wrinkled, Chad looked back at Robin. "This making sense to you?"

"Kinda." Robin shrugged. "I think I understand the issue we're talking about with waves. What I don't understand is why we should care. Even a little. Is this corporate espionage? One group trying to steal scientific secrets from another group?"

"Could be." Isabella pulled up a local map. A pin dropped on a building near the east of the city. "Maybe we need to pay the Stanford Wave Lab a visit to find out."

Robin nodded. "I guess it's all we've got to go on. Who thinks we should check out the wave lab?"

Two hands shot up immediately.

Chad hesitated. "It seems like we're grasping at straws. Just because we found a few people talking about waves, we somehow think that's what the data thieves were after? Rather than some old couple's credit card numbers?"

More nods.

His hand slowly lifted, joining the others.

"All I'm saying is, this lab better have a decent selection of staplers!"

———

Robin wove through the late afternoon traffic, skating.

Even though he had just gotten his driver's license, he still preferred to skate. Driving his mother's car felt like too much responsibility. He didn't like the idea of crashing their one and only vehicle. Even though his mom used public transportation mostly, he didn't want the two of them to have to deal with the possibility of losing their car.

Robin jumped the sidewalk.

The group had agreed to reconvene later that evening. After the majority of the lab staff had already gone home for the night. Hopefully, that would only leave the building's security team and system. That was still a wild card he wasn't sure about. Cameras —most likely. Guards—always a possibility. Armed with real weapons—he hoped not.

Sneaky Inc. hadn't had the time to do the reconnaissance they usually required for this sort of mission. But they were only going to have a peek. To look around and see if there were any more puzzle pieces they could find.

Something to make sense of the data thieves.

His pocket chirped.

DING.

A text message.

He would have ignored it, but it could always be important. About the mission that night.

Robin banked into a narrow alley leading behind a set of tall apartments.

He glanced at his phone's lock screen.

A text from Isabella.

Oh boy. He could feel his heart rate increase. But there was no point in it doing so. This was likely a message about the truck. They hadn't even finished the first coat. The truck looked like an ugly mess.

Swiping up, he unlocked the phone and read:

He was joking, yes?

Her text didn't make sense.

Until it did!

But . . . there was no way she could really be talking about Chad's inappropriate joke. Could she?! His heart hammered away.

Maybe he was wrong. Maybe he had misunderstood her message. That was probably it.

Wiping his palms on his pants, Robin typed a safe response:

Who's he?

There was no immediate reply.

Only those confounded three dots! The ones indicating that the other person was typing.

Robin stared at his screen.

FOREVER!

She knew that was a joke, right? She had to. Chad was always opening his mouth and sticking his foot in it. That *was* Chad!

Isabella had to know the teen had said it just to get a laugh.

Nothing serious!

The three dots suddenly disappeared.

> Who do u think?!

With it was a smiley face winking.

Then another text from Isabella:

> Maybe I feel the same.

Robin could have dropped his phone.

She was playing with him. Toying with him!

Flustered, he clicked off his phone and shoved it into his pocket again.

As deep as it would go!

He didn't like this. His work relationships had to remain professional. Distant!

Chad should have just shut his big, fat mouth. What he said was out of line! And now Robin would need to have a talk with the boy about it. He didn't like that. It felt too much like Robin was the boss of some company and dealing with employee issues. That wasn't the way it was supposed to work.

And then there was the other issue.

The one he quite possibly hated even more than the issue of confronting Chad.

Was Isabella honestly flirting with him?

They were coworkers.

Nothing more!

Robin kicked his board forward.

Extra hard!

Now he would have to say something to Isabella as well.

To stop whatever this was between them—

Before it went any further!

20

obin crouched in the darkest shadows.

Perched one story up, on an unfinished construction site. From the amount of debris lying around, the place looked abandoned. Bags of half-used concrete powder, now hard as a rock.

From this vantage point, he could watch anyone approaching.

The sky displayed the last of its deep navy blue pushing into dark purple. Twilight.

One after the other, the stars revealed themselves.

Robin had darkened his face with hunter's grease. His wardrobe was all black. Tight-fitting canvas pants with lots of pockets. A tactical utility belt designed for law enforcement. A knit black pullover and hood dangled down his back. The hood was just in case he needed to go fully covered. And skintight gloves. Perfectly sized. Made of a thin and supple leather.

And of course his new boots! Having something that nice to wear for once felt good. A splurge, perhaps. But well worth the cost, seeing how it was a business investment. And quite possibly the best one he had made in a while. Unfortunately, the engine inside the food truck was proving to be rather sketchy. Unreliable.

Robin surrounded himself with some of the best gear money could buy. Quality that he could depend on. But now he had to work on himself.

The meeting area, still a few miles away from the lab, was empty.

Robin had wanted to get there early.

He wanted the time to clear his head.

To center his thoughts. To get his game face on.

Every operation the team performed was potentially dangerous. And he needed to remember that.

The one time they got lax and forgot would likely be their last mission.

Then it was back to Burger Barn—

Or worse.

The text exchange that afternoon meant nothing to him now. He had pushed it away.

Robin was in control again.

He just wanted to make sure it stayed that way!

MRRR-RRR.

Out of the darkness, quite possibly the world's ugliest food truck approached.

It looked like the owners couldn't decide if it was still selling cupcakes or—

Delivering milk!

Robin shook his head.

They would finish painting it next week.

There really wasn't a rush to finish it, since the truck's appearance was hardly mission critical.

But Robin still felt it.

The increased heart rate.

The sweaty palms.

That was for the upcoming mission, right?

"Lord, please make this feeling go away," he whispered.

And then a whisper spoke back. *Fully rely on me.*

Hold up. What did that mean?

He'd just prayed. Didn't that mean he was already fully relying on God?!

The food truck pulled up next to the unfinished building and stopped.

Robin stood. He moved toward the end of a long metal beam, balancing his way out over it. He was only maybe ten feet off the ground. Robin liked this kind of heights. Ones that were reasonable!

And with a bit of a jump, he let himself go—

KR-THUNK!

Landing on the roof of the food truck. He yanked open the square hatch on the roof. And dropped inside!

Anika was driving. Go figure.

Chad sat shotgun, playing with a small parabolic mic combo. A clear plastic bowl surrounding a microphone to pick up sounds from a distance.

Robin spun around.

Isabella.

She sat in her computer chair before a glowing bank of monitors.

Robin swallowed hard.

Just as she finished a line of code.

She glanced up at him. Did a double-take.

A thin grin on her face.

Robin lifted a hand in greeting, but spun away just as quickly.

This wasn't the time for any talks. This was just business as normal.

"Alright," Anika said, looking up from flipping through her GPS. "We're only about eight minutes out. Grab a seat, Robin."

Robin looked around.

The food truck had not been fully set up yet.

So much of their time on the vehicle had been spent creating a center floor track that ran the length of the truck. It allowed seats to be mounted inside. From there they could slide back and forth without the threat of falling over during a tight turn.

But it meant there was only one seat available.

The one next to Isabella.

Robin frowned.

———

Anika pulled the food truck in behind an auto parts store and brought it to a gentle stop. Grabbing the shifter, she shoved the vehicle into park.

The store's lights were off. Closed for the night.

The truck wouldn't look so out of place there.

And it gave the team one of the best accesses to the lab.

At least, to the part of the facility that had the least amount of outside lights. Unfortunately, that benefit came with a price.

The reason for so few lights was the large pond between their location and the lab. Clearly manmade. Likely for decoration, considering the fountain nozzles in the center throwing water up into the air.

The Stanford Wave Laboratory itself was a stunning building. Built with all the latest in architectural design, it was clearly a showpiece for the city. Modern steel and glass mixed with traditional brick. It looked more like a college campus building than anything corporate.

And only two stories tall.

Robin was likely happy about that.

To Anika, it merely looked like another job.

And possibly her last.

Especially since receiving the angry text from Robin!

21

With his boots still on, Robin stepped into the feet of a waterproof jumpsuit.

They had ordered these some time ago but never got around to using them.

The suits were hardly anything to speak of in regard to fashion. Nearly transparent, ghostly white, full-body suits. They were baggy and fit neatly overtop of the team's existing outfits. It would be a quick in and out of them.

Just what the situation required.

Robin lowered his shoulders and slid his arms into the sleeves. The cuffs around his wrists were tight and required a bit of maneuvering. But if they truly kept the water out, he wasn't complaining.

ZZZIP!

Robin left the watertight zipper close to his chin, but not too close. He didn't want it to pinch his skin.

Chad strolled up next to him.

CRUNCH, CRUNCH.

The kid was fisting Cool Ranch Doritos into his mouth.

Already outfitted in a full-size suit. Clearly several sizes too big for him.

He looked more like a walking, talking set of window blinds.

"How do I look?" Chad whispered. He held out both arms and did a little twirl.

"You look—you look great," Robin lied.

"Good, because I feel like a transparent raisin," Chad barked, shoveling in more chips. "What, let me guess? They didn't offer these in children's sizes? Why do the little people always get the short end of the stick, huh?!"

Robin didn't let himself laugh.

And he showed little more than a simple grin.

"I'm sorry, buddy," Robin said. "Next time, I'll look to see if they have a version just for you. Granted, it will probably be the Dora the Explorer version, but if you're okay with that . . ."

"Ha, ha. Hilarious. I just want my grievance to be registered somewhere, alright?"

"Duly noted."

"Thank you," Chad said, marching off toward the tall fence that separated them from the water. He unzipped his jumpsuit just enough to reach back into his pants pocket. Producing a quarter, he shielded his face with an arm, then tossed the coin at the fence.

ZRRRTT!

Sparks erupted from the contact!

The quarter never fell away. Instead, it continued to sizzle where it had connected, glowing red, welding itself to the fence.

"Alright, Anika," Chad said casually. "Your turn."

Already in her full-body suit, Anika stepped forward wearing thick black gloves and boots. Rubber. Grabbing a long metal spike and a mallet from her toolbox, she began hammering the spike into the ground.

With that completed, she uncoiled what looked like a set of jumper cables. Only these had one end with a beefy alligator clip while the other end splayed out into a dozen or so smaller clips. A virtual Medusa. She clipped the large end onto the half-buried spike. Moving double-time and using both hands, Anika connected the smaller clips to the individual strands of the electric fence. Clearly, she had done this before. And if bypassing a five-thousand-volt fence ever became an Olympic sport, Anika would definitely be a medal winner.

After attaching the last clip, Anika grabbed another long metal spike from her collection.

Shielding her face, she brushed it against the fence.

Nothing.

With a smile, she poked the metal spike between two horizontal rails on the fence. Pinwheeling the spike, she forced the fence to bunch together in one area while pulling away from another, creating a hole.

Using a spring clamp, she fastened the spike in place.

Finally, using another metal spike and the same technique, she doubled the size of the hole.

Large enough for a human to squeeze through!

As the leader of the group, Robin was going to be first.

He was *not* a fan of electric fences. A nasty form of security, if you asked him. It was too close to making a person into a piece of toast.

Robin knelt and pressed his hands together in front of him.

Such a vulnerable pose.

And in so many ways!

After blowing out the air in his lungs, he pressed himself forward.

Wriggling through the hole.

It was a tight squeeze. Tight enough that they would have to shuttle their backpacks through afterward.

It was difficult work. Wiggling like a worm, with very little to hold on to.

Robin was halfway through when he heard something.

BARK, BARK!

He gasped.

Which only filled his lungs with air. His chest expanded. Pressing it even tighter against the fence!

Dogs! Likely trained to patrol the perimeter. And by the sound of it, only some distance away!

Have no fear, came the whisper. *For I am with you!*

But that felt like cold comfort.

Robin wriggled harder!

Faster!

He was sweating. The plastic jumpsuit trapped his growing heat!

He could hear it louder now.

The gallop of the dog.

Approaching!

And at a faster pace than Robin could manage.

Thrashing about, he jerked both legs forward—

Dislodging several alligator clips.

In those areas, the fence crackled back to life!

And only inches away!

Chad's attached quarter—

Glowed bright red again—

One edge of the metal coin sagged. Until—

One drop of molten metal dripped!

22

Robin was out. Free.

All except one foot—

Caught on the wiring!

"No! Stop!" Anika yelled, grabbing Robin's foot.

Robin clamped his eyes shut.

He didn't want to see what happened next.

Only, he could feel it.

Anika's gloved hand—

Gently guiding his foot through the obstacles.

She carefully unhooked it from where it was caught—

And threaded it through the hole.

GRRRRR!

Robin was on all fours when he opened his eyes.

Staring straight into the eyes of a German shepherd.

A dog that did *not* look like it played nicely.

Robin didn't move.

Everyone froze.

Robin sent up a silent prayer.

Saliva dripped from the corners of the dog's downturned mouth.

Which displayed all its long—

And sharp—

Teeth.

Glistening in the moonlight.

Chad hunched over near the hole. "Hey there, big guy," he spoke in a friendly tone. He was either completely oblivious to the danger they were in or faking it. And rather convincingly at that. "What's your name? Let me guess. Cerberus? Mauler? You know what? You look like your name might be something like Slayer!"

GRRRRR!

The guard dog didn't seem to know where to put its attention.

And what in all creation was Chad doing?!

There was no way this was helping! Did he honestly think he could just make friends with a drooling, snarling—

"Here, try one of these," Chad said, holding something out on the palm of his hand through the opening in the fence.

The dog stopped snarling. It sniffed at Chad's offering.

"Cool Ranch Doritos. Don't get me started on which is better. The original or this kind. That's an honest toss-up, if you ask me. It's debatable."

The dog licked it.

And it apparently liked what it tasted—

Because it quickly gobbled up Chad's offering.

"Here you go, big guy," Chad said, shoving the remains of his bag through the narrow hole.

The guard dog must have completely forgotten about its cornered victim, because—

It attacked the bag, shredding it in the process!

Robin sighed.

His body relaxed. Aching from the tension it was holding.

"Hey, now, don't eat it all!" Chad said, quickly wriggling himself through the hole. "I still want some!" Reaching dangerously close to the dog's sharp teeth, Chad grabbed another handful off the ground. Leaning back, he crunched down on what little remained. Crumbs, mostly. Then licked each finger.

Robin exchanged a look with Anika.

Both of them shook their heads.

———

Robin climbed back to his feet.

"Thank you, Lord," he whispered. "For not letting me fry!"

With Isabella camped out in the food truck, Anika was the last through the hole. Somehow she made it look effortless.

Thankfully, there were no more incidents. At least with the fence.

And as for the guard dog, after his little snack he simply trotted off, seemingly satisfied.

"From what I'm seeing on their outdoor camera feed," Isabella said over Robin's earpiece, "if you continue to approach the corner of the building, you're perfectly positioned in a blind spot across the retaining pond."

The body of water lay before them.

They could march around it. But there were more pole lights in either direction. No—through the water it would be.

Chad hadn't even hesitated. With his suit on, he marched right into the water like it was just another day at the beach.

But when Robin stepped in—

He suddenly felt it.

Ice cold!

He took another step.

And another.

Oh, wow, this was going to be brutal.

Did the lab refrigerate the pond?!

How could it be this warm outside—

And this cold in the water?!

And Robin noticed it. It was hard to tell at first since every part of him under the water felt cold.

But for some reason, it didn't feel like his waterproof suit was working anymore.

He lifted his leg for a better look.

Sure enough, there was a small hole in the leg of his suit.

A melted hole.

From the melting quarter?!

Letting gallons of ice-cold water seep into his suit!

"Problem?" Anika whispered as she approached from the rear.

Robin grimaced. "No, not really." He dropped his leg back into the glacial melt and pressed on like nothing was the matter.

———

But clearly there was a problem!

And Anika could sense it.

What had she done wrong?

If she hadn't moved quickly, Robin would no longer be with them. He would have become a French fry. How could he not respect that?

Not see the value in *her* contribution?

She wanted to ask him about it.

To challenge him, right then and there!

In the middle of a three-foot-deep retaining pond.

But she wouldn't.

Because something was clearly bothering him.

Anika had heard what he said. "No problem." But that's not what his entire demeanor was saying.

And it was likely *all* directed at her!

For something she had done wrong. Why wouldn't he talk to her about it in person? Now it just hung between them. An unspoken problem that Robin had alluded to in his text to her earlier.

And simply would not forgive her for!

23

Thankfully, the team made it out of the water with no more incidents.

But Robin's teeth would not stop chattering.

They peeled themselves out of their suits. Only, Robin seemed to drain about ten gallons of water out of his. And that said nothing about the condition of his lower half.

He didn't speak of it. Kept the stupid mistake to himself. He didn't need the others to lose confidence in him. In their leader!

They pressed themselves up against the least interesting part of the laboratory.

Behind a few well-maintained decorative bushes.

Anika used her battery-powered driver to unscrew a fastener. Catching the screws in her hand, she pulled aside a three-by-three-foot ventilation hatch.

Robin hunched over, one shoe making a squishing sound. He flicked on a penlight.

Pipes.

So many of them. Fat ones, skinny too. All running this way and that.

He glanced over his shoulder. No guards.

It would have to do.

It certainly was no grand entrance to a rather grand building.

But it would work.

And maybe the pipes would offer some warmth.

Robin could only hope as he crawled inside. He used a hand to protect his face from overhead obstacles.

What were they looking for once they got into the lab? Clues, obviously. But would they make themselves apparent?

Or would it simply be another puzzle piece—

That didn't fit the whole?

He'd simply have to wait.

Oh joy.

It wasn't long before the dim tunnel rose up, twisted, and what felt like backtracked on itself. But it all was still going somewhere. Just not in a neat, straight line like Robin wanted. It wasn't difficult to believe the scientific fact that the shortest distance between two points was a straight line. He had adopted that for elsewhere too. For relationships. For his work.

For life!

Except it almost never seemed to actually work out that way.

Why?

Didn't God appreciate efficiency like Robin did?

After all, didn't God invent it?

Create efficiency from nothing?!

So why was so much of life like these claustrophobic utility tunnels?!

Up. Down.

Jerked this way.

Then the other!

Robin wasn't complaining. No. He was simply making a rational and objective observation . . . wasn't he?

There.

Up ahead.

A light at the end of the tunnel.

Rather dim and radiating down from above.

But it gave Robin a goal to work toward. Something that might offer an alternative to shuffling forward like a penguin.

He approached an area where the tunnel widened. It wasn't much—just enough to stand up in. And there, before Robin's face, was a vent. Holding his hand down by his side, he motioned to those behind him by holding up a fist.

There was no way he was going to rush this.

All he needed was one scientist who had stayed late working on some pet project.

Or a janitor halfway through his or her cleaning routine.

No, he could be patient. And would be!

Reaching into a side pocket on his pants, he fished out a small device.

A flexible camera snake.

He plugged it into his phone and, after adjusting his brightness to the lowest levels, he slipped the end of the snake through the metal slats.

Where had they made it to?

The room beyond looked like something out of his biochemistry class. In the distance were workstations with sinks. An emergency eyewash station. Corkboards on the wall along with dry erase boards. Equations that looked completely over his head.

And as far as he could tell—

No people.

Robin threaded the end of the camera back, fitting it with a small mirror adaptor.

With it fixed, he pushed the end through the vent slats again.

He had a new view on the room.

The mirror presented a ninety-degree vantage point.

A good view of the floor. Uninteresting.

He rotated the camera slightly.

A metal trash can. He couldn't see all the way inside it. But from what he could see, it looked empty.

Pulling up on a trigger on the camera, he bent the snake another ninety degrees. He fished the camera farther into the room, finally getting a view of his surroundings above him.

Smaller pipes around him. Hot and cold water. Something that likely was a natural gas feed. And power. All properly shielded. No fear of danger here with that.

Robin slipped the camera back through the vent slats and pocketed the device.

With his latex-wrapped gloves, he gripped the first lever holding in the vent.

He lifted it.

SQUEAK.

Clearly it hadn't been used in a while.

But thankfully it hadn't made much noise.

Robin waited.

To see if anything inside the room reacted.

If anything moved.

And when he couldn't wait anymore, convinced that everything was clear, he pushed it open farther.

The other three latches didn't make noise.

And gripping the vent, lest it should fall out on its own—

Robin carefully—

Slowly—

Slipped a small square piece of felt underneath the vent cover's bottom edge, quietly slid the vent to the side, and climbed out.

Robin paused.

Still nothing.

Sure enough, they had the lab all to themselves.

No cameras.

No motion detectors.

Good!

One by one, the others exited and crawled out from beneath an otherwise typical lab table.

The room felt eerie.

Mostly because a dim combination of red and blue light washed over everything. One color from the emergency exit sign above the door. The other from moonlight through slats in the window blinds.

Various experiments lay strewn about. Mid-use.

Arm-mounted magnifying glasses bringing into clear focus details from circuit boards littered with probes.

Voltmeters with measuring needles swaying up and down.

Thermal measurement devices, their readouts fluctuating.

Oscilloscopes displaying pale-green sine waves.

Robin snapped his phone camera onto his chest harness while pressing his earpiece. "Are you getting all this?"

"I am," Isabella whispered in his ear. "When you're ready, you'll want to head out the door and take a right. Feel free to look around as you go, but I'm leading you to the archives. You'll need to go up a floor to get there."

"Roger that."

Robin approached the lab's exit.

From the inside, he could read the reversed lettering on the glass door: LAB 334.

From the size of the room and the look of things, this was a minor lab. One of dozens, likely. Maybe a temporary work location for visiting scientists. Or a spillover area for temporary projects.

Either way, the team needed to move on.

And quietly.

With his latex gloves on, Robin tried the doorknob.

Unlocked.

Good.

He didn't want anyone to leave anything behind.

Especially fingerprints.

And yet, as he looked down—

He spied something.

A wet footprint.

His own.

It would dry by morning, wouldn't it? But for the next few hours, it was *not* good.

Robin was leaving a trail.

One that led right to them!

24

sabella studied the live video feed coming in from the three cameras when—

DING.

She jumped.

The tension was getting to her. She needed to relax. Everything was going according to plan.

Isabella spun around in her seat.

She was used to having the computers in front of her making noises. One notification or another.

Why was she hearing this from behind her?

DING.

Her phone.

She had it plugged in to charge with one of the several battery banks the truck was outfitted with.

But why was it chirping at her now?

Hadn't she put it in focus mode? Shutting off all notifications?!

A text message.

From her mom.

Where are u?

I'm here at movie theater.

Isabella couldn't understand what she was reading. Why was her mom at the movie theater? And asking where Isabella was?!

"We're at the next intersection," Robin whispered over the speakers—

Catching Isabella amid a text response. She finished typing:

I'm at work!

Spinning around, she grabbed the mouse.

"Hello?!" came Robin's voice again. "Which way do we go from here?!"

"Um, I'm checking now," Isabella said, scanning the blueprints on her screen. "Go left. No, wait! Right. Yes, go right."

She heard Robin grunt. It sounded like frustration.

DING.

She spun back around to her phone.

So you're gonna bail?

DING.

On your mother?

Now it was Isabella's turn to grunt, her fingers speeding over the tiny keys.

I thought movi was nxt wk?!?!

She didn't get an immediate response.

Only three dots.

Isabella tapped her foot.

Why was it taking so long for a reply? What was her mom typing?

A novel?!

"Now where?" Robin whispered.

Isabella whipped around again. And instead of grabbing the computer mouse—

She bumped it.

Minimizing the lab layout window!

"Hold on!" Isabella said. "I'm sorry. I'm having . . . computer issues."

———

Anika rolled her eyes.

Isabella must have been having issues!

Because here they were. In the middle of a massive laboratory. Doing nothing.

Waiting on simple directions!

And with the occasional patrol guard making their rounds.

Sure enough, another guard must have been approaching.

Footsteps.

From their rear!

Anika waved to the boys. With their attention, she cupped a hand around her ear, then pointed behind her.

They needed to pick a direction.

And NOW!

Robin tapped his earpiece. A silent signal to Isabella for help.

"Sorry, I lost the window. Pulling it up now," Isabella said over their earpieces.

Unacceptable!

And Robin didn't wait.

With a slashing hand gesture to his left, he moved in that direction.

All three of them double-timed it.

Hunched over.

Shuffling through the darkness.

Single file.

Taking up the rear, Anika fumed!

Why was her job performance under review—

When clearly Isabella had issues?!

————

DING.

So, I guess that is a no?

Isabella unplugged her phone. She needed it on her workstation. At quicker reach. She typed:

I can't! Wrking!

Isabella eyed the map of the lab again. She wouldn't be caught off guard this time. She had to stay focused.

Only, staring at the main monitor, she was confused.

Hadn't the team gone right at the last intersection?

Or maybe her map had spun around?!

Because their three GPS dots on the map were going in the wrong direction. Where were they?

That wasn't correct.

Was it?!

DING.

On her phone, a sad emoji appeared.

Isabella grimaced. She typed:

> Don't mak m feel wors than i already do!

She adjusted the mic on her headset. "Alright, you're gonna want to take a left at this next intersection."

———

Robin slipped forward to the next intersection.

His one foot continued to squish inside his boot.

Where was Isabella leading them?!

He looked left.

A short hallway.

With nothing more than two restrooms—

And a drinking fountain mounted into the wall.

It looked like a dead-end.

"Left?" Robin whispered. "Are you sure?"

———

DING.

> Sorry. I didn't mean to make you feel guilty. Forgive me. But now I'm wondering if I should just go in and see the movie by myself. Would you be greatly disappointed if I did that? I won't do it if you really want to see it. Otherwise we can watch something else next Saturday night. Maybe with a meal out!

So, now her mom felt the need to write the novel?!

UGH!

Isabella couldn't deal with this.

Not now.

She had explained that she was at work.

Now Isabella was going to do that work and stop responding!

"What do you see to your left?" she asked over the headset.

"Restrooms," came the response.

No, that wasn't right.

Her map was clearly showing a long hallway—

Leading to the building's archives!

25

Robin worked it out by himself.

Deciding that the directional signs in the hallway were more accurate than whatever Isabella was looking at.

He slipped down the hallway with Chad and Anika behind.

They must have simply reworked the building in the last few years.

And never got around to updating the blueprints.

The wall plaque pointed to the archives. Just ahead.

Robin breathed in through his nose.

And out through his mouth.

Nice and slow.

Steadying himself.

His adrenaline was up. Tweaking his judgment. It didn't help when he was short with his teammates.

That was likely true of all of them.

They just needed to relax.

Re-center.

This laboratory was proving to be one of the easiest jobs the team had had in a while. There was no reason to doubt that wouldn't continue.

Robin stopped before a set of doors.

ARCHIVES.

Without a sound, he scanned his surroundings, his back to the doors.

It all looked clear.

And for once Chad hadn't wandered off. A modern miracle?

Robin spun around and gave the set of double doors his full attention. If they were going to find any useful information, it would likely be in here.

Using his penlight, he studied the crack between the two doors. Looking for anything tucked neatly between them. Like a trigger system. For an alarm.

But he saw nothing out of the ordinary.

As Anika stood guard about ten feet away, looking and listening for anything approaching—

Chad laid out a few lockpicking tools on the hallway floor.

Robin turned his attention to the door's hinges.

They were invisible.

Likely on the inside.

But that didn't matter. He scanned the smooth seam between the door and its frame.

Robin looked for small wires.

A thin metal clasp.

Anything that might show a security system at work.

Using one finger, Robin pressed against the fancy high-tech doorknob.

Locked.

Just as he imagined. He shot Chad a thumbs-up and moved aside.

Chad took center stage.

Robin turned his back to the door, taking watch over the hallway farthest away from Anika.

And occasionally glancing over his shoulder—

Checking in on Chad's progress.

———

Isabella glanced at her phone.

The conversation seemed to have stopped.

There were no more messages.

No more dings.

Good. Isabella wanted to keep it that way.

But a part of her wondered.

Curious.

Had her mom gone in and watched the movie?

It didn't really matter to Isabella. Somehow their wires had gotten mixed up. Isabella thought for sure they had scheduled it for next week.

Was Isabella wrong?

She was half-tempted to swipe over to her calendar app and double-check.

But she didn't.

This was a sensitive area for the team.

And she needed to give them her full attention!

———

Wait. Had something just moved?

Anika couldn't quite tell.

If it had, it was subtle. Only the fraction of something.

Likely just her imagination.

An unfortunate byproduct of her occupation.

It tuned all of her senses up to full volume. Maximum load.

She didn't react. Instead, she decided she would give that area extra attention.

But she couldn't tune everything else out in the process.

Until the movement proved to be something more than a shadow—

Everything got equal attention.

And that's when she saw it.

A very faint glimmer of light. A reflection.

Back there in the middle of the hallway. From the direction they had already come.

What was it?

She moved her head slightly.

The glimmer came and went.

Hold up. Something wasn't right.

It almost looked like water.

On the floor!

No. Anika was seeing things.

But when she moved her head again, farther this time—

She saw another glimmer reflecting an exit sign.

That was *not* a footprint, was it?!

And turning around, Anika was just about to scold Chad—

When she saw the puddle.

It was small.

Pooling just under Robin's foot!

Anika blinked.

No. She was *not* seeing that!

She couldn't be!

Not from the one person who was critiquing *her* for not being professional!

———

Robin suddenly noticed Anika staring at him.

Was that a scowl?!

PING, PING.

A tiny screw fell, dancing on the hard, waxed floor.

Chad had half the doorknob disassembled already. Parts of it dangled below, holding on by a colorful ribbon of wires.

An electronic lock!

It sported a twelve-button touch keypad. Zero through nine with the addition of the pound sign and star.

This likely wasn't a big deal for Chad. It merely took more time. And a special sensitivity to it, since security for the door was almost guaranteed at this point.

———

Isabella stared at the video feeds.

Until her eyes hurt from staring!

She looked down for a breather.

And felt guilty.

Isabella shouldn't have been so short with her mom. It was an honest mistake that either one of them could have made. It was no big deal.

Then why had Isabella gotten so upset about it?

In the heat of the moment?!

She would make it up to her mom. What day was it again? They could simply go out tomorrow night. Didn't that work just as well? Sure it did. Isabella would apologize and make it up to her then.

Only, something on one of the monitors caught her eye.

Had she spied movement?

Down the one hallway?

Using the mouse, Isabella pressed the mic button.

But then she didn't say anything.

Isabella clicked it off again.

She had screwed up with the map not so long ago.

She didn't want to mess up again!

26

"Voilà," Chad said. And with a bit of flair, he pushed open the archives' set of double doors!

Robin stood up from his crouched position.

He hadn't exactly needed both doors to be opened. That only drew more attention to them. Ushering the others inside, Robin carefully closed the doors behind them. With the doorknob half-disassembled, he couldn't lock it.

But that didn't matter.

They were now on the inside.

And it was yet to be seen if there were any other exits. The last thing he wanted was to have to go through the entire lockpicking rigamarole again to get out.

They would be just fine inside the archives.

Robin turned around to take it all in.

A vast room. Very much like a library with shelf after shelf of record boxes and cardboard bins, both fat and narrow, likely holding countless reams of data.

Why hadn't an advanced laboratory like this gone digital with their findings?

Or had they, and this was the backup to their digital archives?

Robin remembered losing an entire year of digital photos once. A year of family photos, now gone for good. A year of memories with his father. Robin himself had backed up the photos. Or so he thought. When the computer hard drive crashed, that proved to be incorrect. The images were wiped out. That easy.

How dependent he had suddenly felt on electronics.

On computers.

The greatest invention in the last hundred years, weren't they?!

But how often had they also failed him? Leaving him with a blue screen of death.

And just how much more dependent was he on them now? Or moreso, the whole Sneaky Inc. team?

All of society?!

Maybe the Stanford Wave Laboratory was smarter than them all. By keeping important information on paper, other than in a fire or maybe a flood, it would last forever! Way longer than anything digital.

"Listen up," Robin whispered, gathering the group in a huddle. "For all we know, this could be a dead end. But I wanna give this a look-see. Dig around. It's possible we'll find a clue here that leads to the motive of the data thieves."

"This place is humongous!" Chad blurted, his eyes getting bigger as he looked over his shoulder. "You want us to go through every shelf? Every folder? There have to be thousands here!"

Robin shook his head. "Just look for the most recent entries. Folders that haven't been filed on the shelves yet. New arrivals."

It was a tall order.

A long shot.

But they had nothing else to go on.

The team spread out.

Robin scouted out the main desk area, closest to the archives entrance. Didn't it make sense to start there?

The main desk was a half-circle. It wasn't that much different from the public library near his house. Atop it sat tented signs. INCOMING. OUTGOING.

Robin worked his way around the desk. There were wire baskets holding paperwork. File folders. Charts and diagrams.

He sat on the elevated stool behind the desk and began thumbing through a set of papers.

———

Isabella grabbed an iced tea from the wall-mounted cooler.

This was the boring part of her job.

One where she stared at three little dots on a map. Dots that rarely moved. Her teammates.

And the occasional video feed of documents fluttering past.

The signal was sketchy. Static as much as clean imagery.

She was recording it all. Just in case they needed to dig back through it.

But Isabella couldn't imagine any of it was usable.

Unless . . .

An idea!

With the next clear image of a page on her screen—

Isabella took a screenshot of it.

Pulling up another window, she pasted the image into a program titled OCR.

Optical character recognition.

The entire image became editable text.

Isabella highlighted all the text—

And pasted it into her summary of the stolen cell data.

With a few clicks and instructions into the terminal—

Her software cross-referenced it.

NO MATCHES!

No matter. Isabella smiled. She was on to something!

Without interrupting the live recording, Isabella took all three of the video streams and rewound them. Back to the start of the team's search through the archives.

With one window open for her code, she had the software step through frame after frame of video. Converting and comparing. Data-harvesting everything the team held before them!

With more lines of code, Isabella streamlined the operation.

The computer scanned the frames faster and faster.

Until it was nearly real time!

Amazing!

Her program was able to eat through information at a rate that rivaled an entire army of humans. At the blink of an eye, it could sort and cross-reference an unbelievable amount of data!

Isabella added more to her code.

Tapping into online computer power that quadrupled her own.

The frame rate now moved even faster.

The tiny LED light on her computer processor flickering so rapidly—

It was nearly constant.

Hungry for data, her machine eventually caught up to the live feed. Analyzing everything before it in real time.

Now her software began offering pings. Here and there, matches!

Only, what did that mean exactly?

And that's when she saw it.

On Anika's video feed. Not the paperwork likely occupying Anika's attention—

But the doors to the archives. A bit blurry in the background.

As they slowly opened.

Isabella immediately mashed the Talk button—

Only to meet—

STATIC!

27

Robin was consumed with what he was looking at.

He had seen a few things that raised a red flag.

But he needed more.

More time to review what was in front of him. When—

A hard object worked its way through the hair on the back of his head. Cold and hard. Now pressing against his skull.

"Chad, if you found another rare antique stapler," Robin growled, spinning around, "I'm going to—"

But it wasn't Chad.

The figure, dressed in all black, took a few steps back.

The weapon was still aimed directly at Robin.

"Put down the paperwork," the voice whispered. A female voice. "Slowly now. I don't want any tricks."

Robin did as he was told.

Only, something bothered him.

The voice.

And those hazel-green eyes.

"Wait a minute," Robin said. "You're the—the one!" He couldn't seem to talk. His brain piecing together the memories while reckoning with the front end of the weapon hovering before him. "The one on the cell tower!" He might have said it louder than he was supposed to.

But it didn't look like it mattered. Because just as he went to yell to Anika and Chad—

They both marched up next to him.

Their arms above their heads.

Not sure what to do, Robin's hands quickly followed. Rising above his head.

"I guess I should have locked the door behind us," Chad whispered. "That's my bad."

Another figure circled around behind his teammates.

A male figure.

In an identical outfit. Tight black from head to foot. Utility belt loaded down with what looked like advanced gear. These were no building contractors or night guards, Robin knew that much. These were professionals. And just the villains they were looking for!

Robin burned inside.

They had gotten the better of him and his team.

Again!

"Now, we don't want any problems," the male said, nudging his partner. "We're going to handcuff you and then we can talk about why you're here, alright?"

Without lowering her boxy weapon, the female reached behind her.

Producing a set of handcuffs.

She took a step toward Robin when Chad spoke up.

"Since I already have a hand up, can I ask a question first?"

The female froze mid-step.

The male's eyes narrowed.

Caution radiated in their glances at each other.

"Since you two are armed with nothing more than a few lousy taser guns, I'm wondering if you have the nerve to actually use them?" Chad asked innocently enough.

Robin squinted. Sure enough, they *were* taser guns. Someone had painted over the yellow safety tips on both of them.

"The only reason I'm asking," Chad continued, "is because I've always wondered if it takes the same guts to shoot a taser at someone as it does an actual gun? You know, do people still get shell shock? PTSD?"

The male gripped his taser ever so slightly firmer. Its tip homing in specifically on Chad's chest.

"Go ahead," the male said. "Cuff 'em!"

The female went to move forward again when—

"Because I'm honestly curious enough to do a little test," Chad said, suddenly lowering his hands.

Robin's eyes widened.

His heart hammering away.

Was this a cue?

A prompt for him to act?!

"Oh, do *not* tempt me!" the male snarled, taking a threatening step toward Chad.

"I don't know," Chad continued. "I don't think you have what it takes. For that matter, I bet you've never even jumped down a laundry chute, now have you?"

And for one fraction of a second, the female moved her attention to Chad.

Robin jumped!

Plowing over the female and, with a quick wrestle, yanking free her taser gun.

Haha!

Except it was poor timing. As in the same instant the male redirected his own taser gun and squeezed the trigger—

CLICK.

Two probes rocketed outward, tethered by thin metal wires, and—

K-ZZRRRTT!

Struck Robin square in the chest.

He saw stars!

What he felt was truly not something he could have imagined.

Not as fifty thousand volts screamed through his body!

The pain—

Excruciating!

The complete loss of control. He couldn't move.

Nothing inside him worked!

His arms wouldn't obey. Nor his legs.

Paralyzed!

Every muscle in his body contracted.

Tightened to the point of exploding!

When it all just stopped.

And his body turned to mush.

As he melted into a puddle—

On the ground!

"Okay, I'm wrong," Chad said calmly. "My bad."

28

Anika moved fast.

Before the male figure could break away the end of his used taser cartridge—

And reload!

She lunged next to Robin—

Grabbing the second taser gun!

And rising back to her feet, she trained it on the two black-clad figures before her.

"Here," she said, shoving the taser into Chad's hands. "Hold this on them."

"Whoa there," the male said as the end of the taser gun leveled with his face. "Do you really think that's a smart idea, giving *him* the gun? I mean, do you trust him?!"

"To be honest?" Anika said, taking the handcuffs from Robin's assailant. "No. No, I don't think it's a smart idea." She cuffed the male's hands behind his back. "But when it comes to trust—yeah, I can't count how many times I've had to put my life in those hands." Anika cuffed the female's hands behind her. "And despite my better judgment, so far so good."

Chad sauntered closer to his captives. "Now look who's the new sheriff in town, will ya!" he said, pausing to twirl the taser gun on one finger.

The gun fired.

Sending two prongs up into a hanging bank of light fixtures above.

K-ZZRRRTT!

For a second or two, the lights came on. Shining as brightly as if someone had turned them on.

Then they dimmed again.

"Oh, good to know," Chad said. "Note to self: taser guns have an easy trigger. Don't twirl."

Anika turned to her boss.

The one trying to pry himself off the floor.

She had great empathy for what he had just endured.

Only, she wasn't ready to show it. Not after his text message. Not after he critiqued her "contribution to the team." She still couldn't believe he would write that.

No, Robin could pull himself up!

Meanwhile, Chad grabbed both of his assailants' black hoods and—

WHOOSH!

Yanked them off.

Anika couldn't believe what she was seeing! Two teens. Dark black hair. They were both attractive. And likely the same age as her!

How could this be? The data thieves they had been chasing were no more than high school students? Like them?!

Chad routed through their utility belts like a kid in a candy store. "Oh, you have to check this out!" he said, handing one item after another to Anika. "Seriously. You should see *this* cool thing, whatever it is!"

Anika had no interest in their gadgets. "But—but I don't understand," she said. "Who are you? Why did you come here?"

"Bingo!" Chad suddenly blurted, leaning back. He absorbed with something in his hands. A set of black leather wallets. He flipped them open, reading the IDs. "No. No way. This can't be!"

Chad looked up at Anika.

It was difficult to interpret the expression on his face. Was it shock? Horror? Or merely disbelief?!

Chad could only shake his head.

Then, with a thin smile on his face—

He handed Anika both wallets.

"You are *not* going to believe this!"

———

Robin wanted to die.

"Lord, why did you spare me with the electric fence outside . . ."

Every muscle in his body felt spent. Exhausted!

"Only to electrocute me *inside*?!"

Simply climbing back to his feet took a surprising amount of energy. Energy that he no longer had!

Robin felt wobbly. Had to hold onto something.

And he stared at the boy and girl.

Two Asian teens?

Robin had to fight just to focus his eyes.

Was this the girl that had attacked him on top of the cell tower? As slight as she was, she hardly seemed capable. Or maybe she was more capable than he knew.

Either way.

It was the boy that had electrocuted him.

He couldn't tell if he wanted to punch the kid—

Or cling to him to prevent himself from falling!

Robin chose the latter.

But despite how terrible he was feeling, another part of him wanted to celebrate.

They had done it.

They had successfully captured the data thieves!

Robin laughed.

Sure, it had come at quite a cost. But at least now, Robin could go home. All he wanted was his soft bed to fall into. To sleep! And to hope that maybe in the morning he wouldn't feel so absolutely terrible!

"So, let me get this straight," Anika said, interrupting Robin's thoughts.

She first pointed to the boy. "Your name is Zeke?"

Anika turned to the girl. "And your name is Mia? Brother and sister, is that right?"

They both nodded.

That was nice, wasn't it?

Robin could now give the sibling-criminals names to their faces.

He figured it would look better that way on their mug shots.

When Anika made one more observation.

A little comment, if anything.

One that would have to sit inside Robin's head for a while.

Just to comprehend it.

To fully appreciate the irony.

"And you both work for the CIA?!"

29

obin stared into the eyes of his foes.

Former foes?

Zeke grimaced and pulled his shoulder back, which left Robin to balance on his own.

"No, you can't be serious," Robin snorted, steadying himself. "Are you for real?"

"At least we're working on the side of good!" Mia blurted in Robin's face. "You don't see us trying to steal cell data and sell it for illegal gain, now do you?!"

That was still registering in Robin's toasted brain. When—

"Hold up," Anika growled, getting in Mia's face. "You think *we* stole the data?!"

"Oh, let me guess," Mia said, pointing toward Robin. "This guy was up there atop a cell tower just for the view? Maybe bird-watching? Really?!"

Robin laughed.

Some of the puzzle pieces were finally fitting!

He reached inside his vest to an inner pocket. Unzipping it, he yanked out his own similar leather wallet and, flipping it open, held it out to their two captives.

Zeke and Mia leaned in closer.

Their pupils moving back and forth.

It was Zeke's turn to laugh. "FBI?! No way. I don't believe it!"

Anika and Chad produced similar identification cards and displayed them.

Robin turned to Anika and gestured with his head. "Go ahead, unlock 'em."

As Anika released their handcuffs, Robin leaned in closer to Mia. "You know, I don't know what they teach you in the CIA, but you really didn't have to spray pepper spray right in my face!"

"It was tear gas, if you really want to know," Mia said, the corner of her mouth upturned. "And I don't know what standard procedure is inside the FBI these days, but you didn't have to attack me!"

"Attack you?! I lost my balance, I'll have you know!" Robin blurted. "I don't know if the CIA notified you, but someone was ramming the cell tower we were standing on. I merely reached forward, looking for something to hold on to."

"That might be true, but you didn't need to hold on to *me*!"

"Oh, really?" Robin moved even closer. A scowl on his face. "Then remind me, who was it exactly that held *on to me* when we went over the edge?! Huh?!"

"Alright, alright," Chad interrupted. "Both of you are acting like second graders."

But Robin was good and mad by now. Fuming!

And he had absolutely *no* interest in giving it up!

"Oh, that's rich!" Robin snarled at Chad. "Coming from the second grader who dared that guy—" Robin thrust a finger at Zeke—"to shoot his stun gun at me!"

"This might not be helpful right now," Zeke said, leaning into the conversation. "But technically, it is a taser gun. Just saying."

"ARGHH!" Robin screamed.

He'd had enough of this mission.

Had enough of his teammates.

And he'd most certainly had enough of the CIA! The competition!

Robin marched away.

He ran his fingers through his hair.

He needed a breather.

He needed to walk this off.

The frustration.

The ever-growing complications!

———

Anika decided someone needed to grow up and take control of the situation.

"Alright," she said. "I think we can all get along now, can't we? Yes?" Anika nodded decisively. Then she introduced herself and her other teammates. Finally, she pressed her earpiece. "Isabella, are you there? Are you getting any of this?"

Static.

"Are you communicating with someone outside the building?" Zeke asked. He reached over to the pile of his devices that Chad had collected on the main desk. As Zeke reclipped them onto his belt, he must have found the one he was looking for.

A signal jammer.

Zeke flipped it off.

Suddenly, Isabella's voice came in loud and clear over the headsets. "I repeat, can anyone hear me? Hello? I repeat—"

"Yes, yes," Anika interrupted. "We can hear you now. All is

good. We just ran into—" Anika hesitated. "A few . . . friends," she said with a thin smile. "We can explain more later. Over and out."

Was it cruel to leave Isabella hanging like that?

To use the word *friends* without explaining things?

It would have to do for now.

The team had spent long enough inside the lab.

They needed to find what they came here for.

Or get out!

30

nside the food truck, Isabella sat back.

She forced her shoulders to relax.

Having the others go offline for so long had set her on edge. Her mind had gone off the rails with worry. She didn't like that.

And besides, hadn't the Bible instructed her not to worry?

Except, what if something bad had happened to them?

What if during a mission they were all taken out?

And Isabella was left out in the truck.

Alone.

In the dark.

Not knowing what had happened to the others?!

Double-checking that her mic button was off, Isabella spoke out loud.

"I bind worry and cast it out, in Jesus's name."

She wasn't exactly sure if anything had changed, but she felt better saying it. And within a minute she had forgotten all about those worries. After all, the team had checked in. And Anika had made it clear that everything was alright.

But Anika did say something about running into "friends."

What did that mean?!

And who were the two figures with them?

They almost looked like twins. Could that be?

But how could the team possibly run into friends inside the middle of Stanford Wave Laboratory? And at this hour of night?!

Isabella shook her head.

She didn't enjoy waiting for an explanation.

Probably no more than anyone else.

But that was what she was stuck with.

Isabella turned back to her computer screen. Her programs. And the sorted data it had found. An odd list of what looked like unrelated concepts. There were a few overlaps with the cell data, but not as many as she had predicted.

Except for one word.

HIJENKS.

Isabella likely wouldn't have remembered it from before.

Except for its misspelling.

How odd. What a completely bizarre word to have as an over-lapping result.

Pure coincidence?

TINK, TINK, TINK.

Isabella tapped a beat with a pencil on the keyboard shelf.

Didn't people understand the proper spelling was with an *i* and not an *e*?

Her pencil stopped.

Frozen midair.

She slipped the yellow number-two pencil back into her hair.

Then googled *HIJENKS.*

———

Anika compared notes with Zeke and Mia. "Isabella, our computer genius, ran a copy of the cell data through the wringer. Looking for matches. Similarities. Anything that might trigger an understanding of what the real data thieves were after. But we didn't get much. Just a few repeat terms like *electromagnetic waves* and other wacky phrases. That led us here."

Zeke nodded. "We did something similar. We clearly didn't find what you did, but we discovered a name: Damien Crowe. Apparently, he was a former employee here at the Stanford Wave Lab. And pretty high in command, as far as we could tell. He was fired not long ago. It got ugly and he had to be escorted out by security. Apparently he was caught doing gain-of-function research."

"You mean, like making viruses?" Chad asked.

"No," Zeke said. "This was for modifying a device that Damien's team was working on. Something about the power to seed rain clouds. He thought it could do more than that. Lots more. We don't know much about it beyond that."

"Uh, guys?" Isabella's voice came in over the headset. "You're gonna want to hear this."

Robin stepped closer to the group.

From the looks of things, he appeared to have cooled his rockets a bit.

Or at least, Anika hoped so.

"Go ahead, Isabella. I'm putting you on speaker," Robin said, pulling off his headset.

"Um, hi," Isabella's voice played out loud.

Zeke and Mia waved to Robin's chest-mounted camera.

They couldn't see Isabella, but it didn't take a rocket scientist to understand what was happening.

"What did you find?" Robin asked.

"*HIJENKS*. Do you guys remember finding that word? Well,

guess what? It's not misspelled after all," Isabella said. "It's an acronym."

"An acronym? What does it stand for?" Anika asked. "Or don't we want to know?"

There was a pause before Isabella responded.

"HIJENKS means: high-powered joint electromagnetic non-kinetic strike weapon."

Silence.

Anika's eyes connected with those of her teammates.

Even with those of the CIA duo.

But no one immediately responded.

Everyone was likely processing what they had just heard.

It sounded involved. Complicated.

All but the last word.

WEAPON!

And it wasn't difficult to see where it all might lead.

Because if this Damien Crowe was altering a harmless rain machine into something more—into a weapon!—

That meant that the FBI—

And the CIA—

Were in way over their heads!

31

Robin didn't trust them.

The CIA.

Sneaky Inc. had likely already shared too much. Given away too many trade secrets.

Zeke and Mia might not have been the villains, but they most *certainly* weren't on the same team!

"Alright, well," Robin said, mustering a smile. "Don't let us get in your way."

It was the polite thing to say. Even though his real intent was exactly the opposite. Zeke and Mia could do what they needed to do. But not when Sneaky Inc. was there!

"Oh, trust me, you're not," Mia said, returning some of the attitude. "By the way . . ."

"Yes?!"

"Thanks for the trail of breadcrumbs."

"What?" Robin blinked. He didn't understand her nonsense. "What breadcrumbs? What are you talking about?"

Mia stifled a grin, pointing to Robin's foot. "The trail of wet footprints. I'm sure that saved us a lot of time, at the very least, trying to find the archive room."

She did not just say that!

As far as Robin could tell, his suit leaking hadn't caused any problems.

Did his teammates know about that?!

It wasn't supposed to be an issue.

It was starting all over again. The fight between teams!

And just as Robin pointed an accusing finger at Mia, opening his mouth to fire back something nasty—

KR-THRUMMM!

The entire building shook!

A vibration rippled through the floor. Up into their boots. Into the pit of Robin's stomach.

The archives was mostly devoid of windows. But the few small panes of glass that were there, mounted high on the walls, rattled.

That was not good.

One of the scientists hadn't stayed late just to play with a new invention, had they?

KR-THRUMMM!

This time, the vibrations were more intense.

A nasty crack splintered through one of the windows.

Fragments of glass rained down—

TINK. TINK. CRACK!

Littering the hard floor.

"I think our team has to get out of here!" Robin yelled to Anika and Chad.

"Hold up," Zeke said, grabbing Robin's arm. "I wouldn't go back the way you came."

Robin's eyes narrowed. He yanked his arm free.

"Alright." Zeke shrugged. "It's *your* mistake if you do it."

Robin marched straight for the archives' set of double doors.

And then slowed.

"Why?!" he growled over a shoulder.

"Oh, I don't know . . ." Zeke said, dragging things out.

KR-THRUMMM!

The shaking was only increasing!

Finally, Zeke smirked. "Maybe because we primed several flash grenades and one or two tear gas explosives back there. To keep the security guards busy, you understand. But if you really want more fun, you're welcome to go find them yourself."

Robin and his team were stuck.

At the mercy of the rotten, no-good CIA operatives!

KR-THRUMMM!

Silt filtered down from overhead.

A fragment of drywall steadily separated from the ceiling until—

CRASH!

It fell, crushing a rack of periodicals in the process.

Robin had no idea—

Just how long the building structure—

Might last!

"Or you could just follow us!" Mia yelled over the rain of falling debris.

And that was *exactly* the last thing Robin wanted!

But after evaluating his options—

And looking to the others—

Sneaky Inc. was plum out of them!

"Come on!" Robin yelled to his teammates. "We have to follow them!"

Chad's eyes went wide. "And what if *they don't know* what they're doing?!"

"Then I guess we'll be there to rub it in!"

That wasn't very nice.

But it felt good to say it!

And everyone ran!

Toward the back of the archives room.

As one set of shelves teetered. Rocking back and forth, until one cycle when the shelf tilted just a little too far and—

Couldn't recover!

KR-THUNK, THUNK, THUNK!

Like dominoes, one giant shelf after another plowed over the next!

A flutter of paperwork erupted into the air.

Using his arm, Robin covered his face. He wove his way down the only remaining aisle, threading through the wreckage!

To a single door at the back of the room.

An exit?

Zeke and Mia seemed to be basing their escape plan off a sheet of paper. A map? How did the CIA get that? And more importantly, *why didn't* the FBI have that same information?!

The walls strained against themselves, warping and distorting the shape of the room. Zeke didn't hesitate. He shouldered his way through the door, busting the lock in the process.

Robin could have done that.

It wasn't some heroic act of strength.

Likely it had been a flimsy lock!

Everyone raced into the back room.

The area was tight, cramped with supplies. Stacks of empty file folders. Broken file racks waiting to be fixed. Even an intern desk piled high and a laser printer.

But it was what scaled the back wall that caught everyone's attention.

A metal ladder built into the wall.

A fire escape?

Or roof access for the maintenance team?

No one questioned it.

As Zeke kindly let his sister go first and then ushered each of the Sneaky Inc. team up, one at a time.

Except Robin lingered toward the rear.

KR-THRUMMM!

And when it came his turn, Zeke offered for Robin to go ahead of himself.

Only, Robin wouldn't have it. Instead, he gestured for Zeke to go first. "No, no. I insist!"

"We don't have time to argue!" Zeke growled. "After YOU!"

Robin was determined to go last. After all, he was in charge, even if it was of nothing else than himself! And he didn't need some *other* wannabe leader of some *other* team trying to be artificially courteous and kind when *clearly* the real issue was—

KR-THRUMMM!

Another loaded shelf rocked off its stable base.

A wall of thick hardback books dumped outward—

Causing both boys to jump for the ladder—

At the same time!

32

sabella minimized the live video feeds.

Because if she didn't, she would throw up!

She never liked this part of the missions.

When everyone was running.

When the world looked like it was falling apart around them!

First of all, it was stressful to watch. Isabella really couldn't do anything to help them when everyone was screaming. When the cameras bobbed up and down, spitting out all sorts of unviewable footage.

No, she had better ways to help her team.

Like begin scouring the laboratory's security feeds. To figure out what was happening!

And what Isabella might do about it.

If anything!

And that's what she was doing. With her fingers a blur over the keyboard—

She was flipping through every fixed camera view inside the entire facility.

And there were a lot of them!

ROB BADDORF

One after the other, she looked for the source of the problem.

But she wasn't finding it.

At least, not quickly.

All Isabella could find were images of the security staff within the building—

Trying to find stable footing. Falling over!

Desperate to understand the attack themselves!

———

Anika was the first of the FBI to make it through the square hatch in the ceiling.

Out onto the rooftop.

There was the incredible hum of the rooftop heating/cooling units blowing away like jet engines. Loud enough that Anika's first response was to shove her hands over her ears.

But for a brief moment, everything *looked* peaceful.

Another lovely night with very few clouds in the sky.

Which presented her with a vast view of the stars.

And the galaxy holding them together.

Had they really just arranged themselves there?

By accident?

KR-THRUMMM!

When the terrible, dreadful sound came crashing through her momentary bliss.

Anika spun around.

Just in time to witness a massive force drop down from nowhere and strike the rooftop!

Instinctively, she reached out to steady herself against an air duct.

What was that thing?!

At first, the object reminded Anika of an upside-down

Christmas tree. But this thing was big. Much bigger than the trees her family would cut down for the holidays. This was closer to the size of the tree the YMCA would set up. In their oversize lobby!

A giant drill head!

There was no pointy tip on this device. In its place were three smaller drill heads. Spherical. Each one was several yards across in size. All rotating. Intertwining and mashing their beefy cogs between each other.

A veritable meat grinder!

After every strike on the rooftop, the entire object rotated.

Grinding itself further through the metal beams and sheeting that made up the rooftop. Its metal teeth tearing up everything in its path!

And that's when she spied it.

It was almost invisible in the dark.

A thick cable.

It held the drill head aloft from somewhere high above.

Anika tilted her head back.

Silhouetted by the night sky, an enormous helicopter hovered some distance above. It sported dual rotors.

Were the helicopter sounds intermixing with the building's already-deafening HVAC system?

Mia pressed her head in close to Anika's. "It's a Boeing CH-47 Chinook!" she yelled just loud enough to be heard.

The twenty-foot-long drill abruptly groaned and stopped rotating. It was caught up in the tangle of twisted roofing materials.

The drill head rose into the air again. Only to—

KR-THRUMMM!

Strike again. And with such force!

There was no way the building could withstand such a beating.

Not for much longer!

Robin scrambled up and out of the hatch.

He wasn't the last one out of the building. But that didn't matter. It wasn't a competition.

His eyes widened as he spied what the others were witnessing.

Anika spoke directly into Robin's ear. "Boeing helicopter! CH-47 Chinook!"

Robin nodded.

Clearly, their hunch about the Stanford Wave Laboratory was correct.

Now if only they could stop whatever was happening!

Robin knelt, slinging off his backpack. As he did so, he went through a mental inventory of his tools.

Did he have anything to stop a helicopter?

Or a twenty-ton drill head from burrowing into a rooftop?

Robin went to unzip his pack, but he already knew the answer.

He had nothing.

He wasn't prepared. Not for something like this!

Pulling off his own slimline backpack, Zeke knelt down beside Robin.

Zeke unzipped his bag, pulling out different tubes and pipes.

He began screwing them together, making one long device.

"If you ask me," Robin yelled, leaning closer to the teen boy, "I'd say that looks like a Boeing CH—um . . . 58—"

"A 47 Chinook?"

"Yeah, maybe!" Robin shrugged. "I still think it could be a 58!"

Zeke grinned as he snapped a narrow wooden stock onto the back of what was rapidly becoming a wide-mouthed rifle. Reaching back into his bag, he slapped what looked like two oversize bullets into the back of the weapon. Then he pointed the assembled rifle skyward.

Directly at the helicopter!

"Hold up!" Robin yelled. "You're not actually going to shoot it —knock it out of the sky—are you?!"

Zeke didn't respond.

Closing one eye, he aimed down the metal sights—

And pulled the trigger!

33

LOOPH!

The projectile soared heaven-bound!

Speeding directly for the nose of the helicopter, when—

PLOOMM!

It exploded in a cloud of thick gray smoke!

With his mouth hanging open, Robin turned to Chad in awe.

Chad turned at the same time. Their expressions perfectly mirroring one another's.

They *had* to get one of those!

And somehow Robin knew that despite all the activity around them, including the caving-in of the roof, that a smoke grenade launcher was likely already in the team's Amazon cart, with Chad smashing the Buy Now button!

Blinded, the helicopter took evasive maneuvers, arcing to one side.

The massive drill head, its three tips still spinning, dragged behind it.

Now careening in their direction!

Destroying—grinding!—everything in its path.

Okay, so maybe the CIA didn't have all the best ideas!

The group frantically divided.

Diving out of the way, face-first, onto the rooftop.

Just as the drill head—

SWOOSH, SMASSSHH!

Skipped past, obliterating everything in its path.

Heating, ventilation, and air conditioning machinery exploded!

Metal shrapnel flying in every direction!

The drill head finally cleared the rooftop—

Leaving a nasty scar of wreckage in its wake.

With the rooftop HVAC machinery destroyed and the helicopter moving away, a general quiet came over the area.

Members from both teams began climbing back to their feet. Checking themselves for any damage.

There were OK signs all around.

"It looks like it's circling," Anika said, pointing to the sky. "I don't think we want to be here for round two!"

"Alright, but where do we go?!" Mia yelled.

Robin looked back at the hatch they had just come up through.

The former hatch! Because the drill head had mashed the metal door back onto itself.

Giving it everything he had, Robin pulled up on it.

No go!

The twisted metal wouldn't even budge.

They'd have to find another way.

Another way off the roof!

———

Isabella found something.

It might not be a solution, but it was certainly interesting.

She leaned in closer to the lab's security feed in one of the central design areas. It was a room much like where the team had entered, but twenty times larger. A workspace for bigger projects that likely required more staff.

And interestingly enough, there must have been a sizable project.

Squarely in the center of the room.

Only, the security cameras wouldn't show it.

Not properly. The center area of the room was pixelated.

And if that wasn't strange enough—

Isabella had been watching silt and debris from the ceiling fall into the room and become pixelated. Almost as if someone or something was on the roof, boring into that area specifically.

And now the drill—if it was that—had stopped. Gone.

Did the rest of the team know about that?

She pulled up the Sneaky Inc. live camera feed.

Sure enough, Anika was dusting herself off and pointing up to the nighttime sky.

At what exactly?

The voice feed was mostly coughs and groans.

The video itself was dark. Not the best cameras for low light.

But it looked like maybe a helicopter approaching.

And quickly at that!

She mashed the Talk button on the screen. "Robin, can you hear me?"

More noise. The response was little more than a mash-up of different voices. All talking over themselves. Arguing?!

"Robin, can you hear me?!"

"No time," Robin responded. His voice suddenly sounded close to the mic. Intimate. "We need to find a way off the roof! Can you help us?!"

"The hole," she yelled. "In the roof! Run over to that!"

"Roger that!"

And just as quickly, the conversation went dark.

Isabella moused over and turned on an Internet radio station quietly.

Smooth jazz.

Isabella pretty much hated what sounded like a doctor's office. But she needed something that would make her chill out!

"God, please help me to relax," she prayed. "And help save the others!"

If everything went well, any second now she should see her friends on the security camera.

As they entered the large lab room from above!

34

The entire group raced toward the gaping hole.

Robin watched as Mia fiddled with her own gun-shaped tool along with a spool of thin cable.

Like a runner sliding into home plate, Mia slid to a stop inches from the hole the drill had created.

She didn't waste even an ounce of movement.

With her long-barreled pistol already pointed down onto the rooftop.

F-TOOMPT!

A concrete nail gun!

With several steel eyebolts already firmly embedded.

The giant helicopter and swinging drill head continued their approach!

Holding onto one end of the cable, Mia tossed the spool down into the hole.

She fed the thin, twisted cable through a few loops on her belt—

And then jumped. Backward!

SWIZZZ!

And just like that, Mia was gone.

Down into the jagged hole!

As Chad and Anika followed suit, threading the cable through their belts and descending, Robin leaned forward. He wasn't sure if he really wanted to look. Maybe it was better not to know what lay ahead of him?

He peered over the edge anyway.

Yup. He should *not* have looked. That was a mistake.

"You first!" Zeke screamed as he threaded the cable through Robin's utility belt. "I know what I'm doing and will bring up the rear!" Lastly, Zeke clipped a descent controller onto the wire.

Neither option actually sounded good.

How big was the drill head again?

From the corner of his eye, Robin spied it. As it smashed into the side of the building on its return!

"Um, no!" Robin blurted. "I might go a little slower than you and don't want to—"

But he didn't have time to finish.

Not before Zeke shoved him!

And Robin spiraled!

Straight down.

Until the descent controller kicked in.

B-ZZZZZ!

Slowing him to a nice and gentle speed.

Robin gritted his teeth.

If he had the chance, he was *definitely* going to kill Zeke!

At least, after Sneaky Inc. ordered the same devices!

Robin's feet gently touched ground.

As he steadied himself, he tried to yank off the descender and the cable. But he had no idea how they worked and couldn't break free. If anything, his efforts were only making things worse.

Mia stepped forward and easily unclipped him.

Wait, did she just roll her eyes?

Like he was a beginner?!

But Robin had to move.

Or be crushed by Zeke! Who apparently didn't need the descent controller and came down like a rock!

"This is it!" Anika yelled over the din of the returning helicopter. She pointed beside them to a large workstation positioned in the center of the room.

It looked like a custom-made table with ventilation and all sorts of electrical ports built right into it. And atop it, held aloft, was a single missile-shaped object.

The missile had a tapered nose cone and sported four narrow fins at the rear. In the center of the missile's body, it had an open hatch. And inside that nestled a smaller device: half shiny metal and half some sort of clear polymer. From what could be seen, it was filled with a glut of all sorts of electronics. Circuit boards. Miniature computer parts. And a network of thin wires connecting it all.

Robin wanted to touch it.

But thought better of it.

They claimed this thing was scientific? Supposed to make rain?

Who did that fool?!

From the looks of it, there was no confusing its clear, weapon-like appearance.

"Help me transfer it!" Anika yelled, shoving one end of the missile case onto a rolling cart. The group all helped. Yanking cables and pipes and disconnecting it from the workstation.

Was this a smart thing to do?

What if it needed a cooling system connected to it at all times?

Just then, a set of half a dozen black ropes dropped around them.

171

That only made the two teams work harder. Faster!

But it wasn't enough.

The missile was crazy heavy. And the weak cart threatened to dump the load or be crushed underneath it if they transferred all the weight onto it.

THUNK. THUNK. THUNK.

Heavy combat boots hit the ground around them.

And more than one pair.

"Don't move!" came the stern command behind them.

"Or we *will* shoot!"

35

Helpless, Isabella saw it all before the first of her teammates even spun around.

The five mercenaries had rappelled down behind them.

Never once taking their hands off their weapons.

Adults. Clearly all male. Outfitted in dark outfits topped with bulletproof vests and other assortments of body armor. They each wore a darkened kevlar combat helmet equipped with a mix of supplies. Flashlights. Night vision. Yellow-tinted visors extended down over their eyes.

And all carried powerful armaments.

FN SCAR and STA-52SE automatic rifles.

Hadn't Isabella's friends heard them coming?

Or even seen them?!

Well, it was too late now.

All work put into moving the pixelated device—whatever it was—stopped.

The FBI raised their hands. And whoever it was with them did the same.

All except Robin. What was he doing?!

His one hand seemed to dip. It lowered, as if reaching for something.

Did he not understand the severity of the situation?!

————

Robin glanced up.

He could just make out the twin rotor blade overhead.

And he had no problems hearing it or feeling its wind on his face and through his hair.

But there was no drill head hanging at the end of the thick cable.

Had they disconnected it? The massive drill head now must be laying abandoned on the rooftop. It was a wonder the roof could still hold it.

In its place was a crane hook. Much smaller and more reasonable.

An individual rode down on it, tightening the bolt with a long wrench as he descended.

The person looked muscular. But he didn't dress like the mercenaries.

Robin had to laugh.

Because the figure almost looked out of place.

Dressed like a common farmer!

No—more like a woodcutter. A lumberjack, once he slung the wrench over one shoulder.

The man wore a red-checkered shirt and blue jeans. But it was the suspenders that topped off the outfit.

As the hook touched the floor, the man stepped off of it.

"My, my. Working late? The laboratory sure is hiring younger and younger these days," he said with a jovial laugh. "I have to wonder if you aren't my replacements here. But where are my manners? Let me introduce myself. I am Damien Crowe. A former employee here. Senior vice president, if titles even matter to you."

Robin inched himself closer to Zeke while subtly reaching for something. He eyed Damien. The man's rusty-brown thick hair. The full beard and mustache. He didn't exactly look the part of a scientist.

But then again, what was a scientist supposed to look like?

The stereotype of glasses and a white lab coat?

A pocket protector?

Damien wore glasses that had been old-fashioned—thick and black on the top, gold wire at the bottom—but were popular now. A retro-cool look. Definitely not something Robin was expecting.

"Titles mean nothing to *me* now," Damien continued, strutting toward the HIJENKS device. "They are only used to separate those with power from those who have none," he said, running a finger over the sides of the sleek machine. "A pity, really. Yet another example of how we have let our own creation turn around and rule us. The *spark*"—he used air quotes to emphasize the word—"leading to our own destruction." Damien gazed down at the missile, lost in thought. "But not anymore," he whispered.

Robin shuffled another inch.

Behind Zeke.

Sure enough, Zeke still had the smoke grande launcher assembled.

Clipped and dangling from his belt!

If Robin couldn't stop Damien—

Maybe Robin could steal it first!

Sure, the device was crazy heavy, but they hadn't really had the chance to test it out on the cart. Robin was convinced it would hold.

And taking a deep breath—

Robin reached!

He knew he would never get the grenade launcher unclipped in time. That was never his goal.

Simply reaching the trigger was all Robin was after.

And before any of the mercenaries noticed—

He got to it!

FLOOPH!

36

LOOMM!

The smoke canister ricocheted around, spewing clouds behind it. The thick white smoke quickly consumed Robin and the others. Big billows formed. Filling most of the room!

There were coughs and gags!

Robin had no time to waste.

Any minute the mercs would open fire!

Robin lunged for the HIJENKS device.

Now that he was working alone, it would be easier.

Robin could pull the device onto the cart all by himself, couldn't he?

Only, as his hands groped about, feeling for it—

He couldn't find it.

As if it simply wasn't there!

Had he misjudged the distance? He stepped forward again and again, his hands leading the way. But now he couldn't even feel the workbench.

Or the cart!

And the more he corrected his orientation—

The more disoriented he became!

Robin felt something warm and squishy.

"OW!" a voice near him yelled. "Someone poked my eye!"

This wasn't working.

And—cough, cough!—the smoke wasn't getting any thinner.

That's when someone grabbed his wrist!

———

Anika found the door first.

And it was a good thing, because if Damien's thugs hadn't killed them yet—

That awful smoke would!

Chad had stumbled out of the plume first. When he caught sight of Anika motioning with her arm, he quickly exited along with her.

But where had Robin gotten to?

And was the FBI responsible for rescuing the CIA?

Anika didn't know. She'd never believed those two alphabet organizations would ever be in the same room!

There!

Anika saw the wet bootprint first—

Then the boot squishing out water!

Anika reached into the cloud—

And grabbed Robin by the wrist!

She pulled, directing him out the lab door and back into the dark maze of hallways. Anika pressed her earpiece. "Isabella, get us out of here! And pronto!"

"On it," came the reply. "Take the first hallway on your left and then turn right!"

Anika and Chad were running now.

But Robin lingered.

Back by the doorway.

"I need to go back in there!" Robin yelled. "I couldn't find it in all the smoke. I have to try again!"

Anika and Chad stopped.

"Forget it!" Chad chirped. "We're outgunned. Let's get out of here so we can fight another day!"

But the expression on Robin's face looked sad.

Like disappointment.

"But—but . . ."

Anika jogged back and took her boss's hand.

She didn't want to. She was still plenty mad at him.

But this wasn't the time to be petty.

Instead, she gently tugged on his hand again.

Robin came along without any resistance.

Anika could only hope that Zeke and Mia made it out okay. She wasn't looking to expand the babysitting job she already had. But she also didn't want them falling into the hands of a hip-fashion madman. Or whatever this Damien character really was!

Soon enough, Robin ran of his own volition.

Anika dropped his hand—

As they obeyed Isabella's instructions and rounded the next corner.

Only, it ended all too quickly. Another dead end!

A space for storing bundles of toilet paper and hand sanitizer.

Why did Isabella lead them here?

Especially when they might have guns chasing them?!

"No-go," Anika said as calmly as she could, pressing her earpiece. "Do you not see where we are?!"

———

Isabella saw exactly where they were!

And the hallway in front of them was completely open, clear.

The quickest way to the exit.

Why couldn't *they* see that?!

"I'm sorry!" Isabella cried, her shoulders slumping. "I don't know what to do—it looks like my map is out of date. I'm afraid you're on your own."

No response.

Isabella watched the three glowing dots move about.

Walking through walls.

And taking turns that didn't even exist.

At least, not on the blueprints she was seeing.

———

"I think we should go this way," Chad said, pointing.

"No, I say the exit is *this* way!" Robin argued.

"Why do we always do what *you* want to do?" Chad growled. "Is it because you have the important job title?!"

Robin's eyes narrowed.

"We're not actually going to have an argument about this here," he said sternly. "Are we?!"

Chad backed down. Looking at the polished floor, he shook his head, kicking at an invisible spot.

Anika shook her head too.

"Good!" Robin barked. "Because the last time I checked, I was still the leader of the group. So, for right now, I'm going to lead, alright?!"

Robin knew they had to get out of there!

But he gave it an extra moment before moving again. Just to let his meaningful words really sink in.

"Good. So we're going my way!" Robin said, jogging ahead.

When it hit him. Literally.

THWAP!

Apparently Robin hit the tripwire of one of the CIA's booby traps.

BLAAANGG!

And a flash-bang grenade!

37

With his head in his hands, Robin slumped on the back bumper of the food truck.

Trying to blink away the bright spots in his vision.

And to hear again.

In one sense, he was hearing just fine.

But he only heard one thing.

RIIIING.

A terrible, high-pitched squeal.

It was things like human voices and car traffic that he still couldn't hear. Not well. Muffled. Consumed by the constant hum as his hearing slowly restored itself.

Where had it all gone wrong?!

Robin couldn't understand it. And he was tired of trying to figure it out.

On his own!

Where was God in all this?!

And why wasn't Robin getting the wisdom he needed to make things right?!

He was tired of waiting.

If anything, Robin was ready to quit. Go back to flipping burgers. Burger Barn hadn't been all that bad, had it? At least there he never got tear-gassed. Or tasered. For that matter, he couldn't once remember having a flash-bang go off in his face while dropping the French fries down into the grease.

———

Robin's position didn't change.

He was still sitting, slumped over, his head in his hands.

Only the setting changed.

Where was he again?

Robin wasn't paying attention—still lost in thought.

Pastor Peter plopped down in the seat beside him. The adult remained silent and merely slipped an arm around Robin's shoulders.

Robin looked over and grinned. It wasn't very convincing, but for now it was the best he could offer.

And knowing Pastor Peter, he could read through anything.

The evening service was long over. Except for stragglers, they were the only ones who remained near the back of the church, in the young adult room.

They sat there for a while, just like that—

Before Robin eventually cracked. "How long?" he whispered. "How long do you have to wait for God to do something?"

Pastor Peter nodded slowly, as if taking in the weight of the question.

Robin studied the man's tattoos. On his forearm were a myriad of illustrations. A pile of rocks. A set of stone tablets. A dark and empty tomb—the stone in front of it rolled away. They were all intertwined. Artistic. Illustrating one thing or another from the Bible. The Old Testament on one arm. The New Testament on the other.

"That's a tough one," Pastor Peter eventually said. "It seems like so often God's timing has nothing to do with our own."

"You can say that again."

Now it was Pastor Peter's turn to grin. "Sometimes God's timing is at work before we even know it. Before we pray for His interaction. For His help. Other times, God seems to wait for what feels like forever."

Robin nodded.

"God told Abraham he would have a child," Pastor Peter said. "You know how long Abraham had to wait? Twenty-five years."

"I haven't waited that long yet," Robin said with a growing smile.

"I didn't think so. Other promises take even longer, you know. The book of Hebrews talks about some who were faithful to God but who died without receiving the things He promised. It says they had to see those things from afar." Pastor Peter paused. "Are you prepared to wait that long?"

Robin lifted his head and sat back up.

He hadn't thought about that.

About the fact that things might not all be resolved on his watch.

That not only might Robin go the rest of his life with a fear of heights—

But also that Damien Crowe might not come to justice.

At least, not while Robin was still alive.

He swallowed hard.

That was a difficult truth to accept.

But he also knew the right answer.

"Yes," Robin whispered, chewing on his lip. "And no, at the same time, if I'm being honest."

Pastor Peter's grin grew into a smile. "I hear you. I can relate, trust me." He tilted his head back and yelled toward the ceiling. "Lord, we believe! But please, help our unbelief!"

38

I t was late when Robin made it home.

With his mom asleep, he tiptoed up the stairs.

He passed his bedroom door and padded his way into the bathroom. Turning the doorknob, he edged the door closed, making sure the latch didn't make noise.

Lashed together by their laces, his new boots hung upside down over the tub.

Robin flipped on the lights over the mirror.

And turning back to his new and most favorite boots ever, he felt them. The outsides were nicely dry. He cringed as he looked at just how much of the sole on both of them had already ground itself off from the parachute landing.

Oh well.

What really mattered right now was on the inside. He reached in as far as he could and felt around.

Robin frowned. His brow knitted down into his eyebrows.

Still wet.

Rats!

Why hadn't they dried out yet?!

Robin dug around inside one of the sink drawers to find a hair dryer. He plugged it in, his thumb hovering over the on switch.

Robin scowled even more.

He couldn't turn it on. The hair dryer would make too much noise. And at this time of night, there was no way his mother wouldn't hear it.

And then there'd be the interrogation. "Why were you out late? How did your brand-new boots get damaged? And so soon?!"

Robin yanked the power cord from the outlet.

No, they would have to dry on their own.

Great.

One more thing Robin could add to the list of things he was waiting on!

———

The next day, the entire gang was back at the team's headquarters.

Isabella sat at the desk in front of her laptop. She tapped a pencil against her leg.

Anika perched off to the side, folding a sheet of paper into a boat.

Chad picked at a stale cupcake. His legs worked themselves back and forth as he sat on top of an abandoned grocery shelf up against the far wall.

While Robin looked up toward the ceiling.

He was pacing again.

In his everyday sneakers.

Despite hanging up the entire night, his boots were still not dry.

But he had other things on his mind right then. And pacing was the best way he knew to keep himself busy—

While concentrating.

Thinking!

His back-and-forth path had already made a new clean spot on the floor—

When he paused.

His head suddenly turned back toward the others.

"Spark," he said.

His teammates broke from their own deep concentration, their eyes focused on him.

Waiting for more.

But it didn't immediately come.

Silence.

Finally, Robin spoke again. "'The *spark* leading to our own destruction.'" He made the air quotes with his hands. "Why did the guy emphasize the word *spark* there? Did that seem odd to anyone else?"

Chad shrugged and shook his head.

Anika and Isabella looked at each other.

They weren't getting anywhere.

"What did Damien say just before that?" Robin asked, moving closer. "Something about letting our own creation . . . "

"Turn around and rule us," Anika said, finishing the quote.

"That's right," Robin said, absentmindedly pointing toward Anika. "Isabella, can you do a search for the word *spark*?"

Isabella inched her seat forward, closer to the desk and laptop. But her fingers didn't connect with the keys. "One word? That's gonna be too broad. We'll get billions of hits."

"Alright." Robin leaned in over her shoulder, toward the screen. "Add the word *HIJENKS*. Misspelled, of course."

Isabella did.

But the results were lean. It looked like there was little to no connection between the words.

"Try *spark* and the word *creation*," Anika said.

Isabella's fingers banged out the search terms.

But she shook her head. "I'm still not getting anything that looks useful."

Robin looked up at the ceiling again.

They were close—onto something!—he could feel it. But what search term were they missing?

"Try *spark* and *pound cake*!" Chad blurted with a laugh. "That was on our list from the cell data. I remember it because it made me think of my grandmother's pound cake!"

Isabella's eyebrow rose. Doubtful.

But she typed it in anyway.

"Whoa." Her eyes went wide.

All of theirs did!

"Get a load of this!" Isabella said, pointing at the screen. "A new artificial intelligence named Spark, formerly known as Pound Cake, goes live!"

"No way," Anika said, skimming the article. "You've got to be kidding me. Programmed by a company named Luminous Data. And wow, get a load of this: the company's value has already quadrupled with the release of the newest version."

Robin took a step back from the others who were all squeezing in to read more.

It was getting too tight for his comfort.

And too hot.

So, Spark it was!

Artificial intelligence.

But wasn't AI just software supposed to help humanity? Be an assistant in everyone's pocket?

Maybe Damien was simply needlessly worried that the sky was falling.

Or was he onto something?

Something more sinister.

A darkness.

When scientists' own creation would turn around—

To rule the world?!

39

A tiny icon blinked. In the upper right-hand corner of Isabella's screen.

She clicked on it.

A new window popped up.

A warning message.

Isabella had coded this alert system herself. A scanner of sorts —one that read through all of the city's emergency broadcast systems. It scanned for things. Keywords that might be of interest. Things generally out of the ordinary. Catchphrases like *terrorism*, *explosion*, or *mass panic*.

Her alert had apparently triggered multiple phrases at once.

Isabella knew that the best way to handle a crisis was to remain calm.

To go suck on a lollipop, as her CPR instructor once said.

Not that you wanted to waste time. Oh, no.

But you needed to keep yourself chill. So that you didn't become part of the emergency yourself!

Using her mouse, Isabella shut off the alerts.

She turned her attention instead to the broadcasts coming from the various local news organizations. Her screen quickly filled with a grid of different live broadcasts.

Except they weren't all that different.

For some odd reason, each and every video feed displayed the same thing.

An image of Damien Crowe, wearing a brown-checkered shirt this time.

His mouth was moving.

But there were no words.

Not until Isabella unplugged the headphones she had left lying on the desk.

"—and I'm sorry to interrupt your morning talk shows," Damien said in a rather cheerful tone. "But I have something a little more urgent."

Hearing the man's voice again grabbed everyone's attention.

With all the local news organizations offering the same footage, Isabella clicked on one at random.

The tight shot on Damien Crowe filled the screen.

"From the way I see it, humanity has crossed a line," Damien continued. His tone of voice turned more serious. "A line that we will not be able to cross back over when things turn bad. Oh, and they will turn bad, trust me. I've spent a good portion of my life studying and helping to advance these same technologies. I know what these machines are capable of. I've seen firsthand what artificial intelligence can offer us. I'm telling you now, they need to stop! And more specifically, the usage of Spark AI needs to STOP!"

Silence.

For a moment, Damien said nothing more. He let his words sink in.

And no one from the Sneaky Inc. team said anything.

It was as if the video had mesmerized them. They sat entranced!

Not just by the words of a criminal who had destroyed a major laboratory the night before.

But by the fear that he was pointing to something worse.

A prophet of impending troubles?

Or merely the ramblings of a dangerous madman?!

Isabella couldn't say.

There certainly appeared to be something to what the man was saying. An unsettling truth that he pointed to. One that stuck in Isabella's throat.

Damien was raising questions. Ones that Isabella couldn't easily answer. And of anyone in the group, she was the one who should be able to. Isabella loved computers! They were her hobby. Her occupation.

And sometimes when she was at her most lonely—

Even a close companion.

"Stop the advancement of Spark AI now!" Damien continued, his voice only intensifying. "Or my team and I will cut it off at the head. And I cannot promise you there will not be collateral damage when we do it. I don't want to see anyone else get hurt, but there is a cost to pay when we play god! You don't understand what this kind of software is capable of. Or how it is advancing on its own. By leaps and bounds. An even greater price will come due upon humans if Spark is not deactivated now—before it enslaves us all!" Damien narrowed his eyes and stared directly into the camera. "You have one hour to comply. Do not be deceived. AI is already a part of your life, controlling aspects that its inventors don't even understand. Every day it grows stronger. Stop it before it grows too powerful to stop. Stop it before it's too late!"

The image from the live broadcast flickered.

It bent, distorting itself.

And then was gone.

Some old game show rerun resumed. On screen, the contestants were clapping and laughing. Winning sponsored prizes and having fun while doing it.

Isabella clicked the window closed.

The air inside the grocery store felt oppressive.

Heavy.

Was Damien Crowe prepared to use the HIJENKS weapon to stop AI?

And if he was, what did it even do?!

It almost felt like the end of the world . . .

Again!

40

sabella heard the speech.

Now if she could only figure out what it meant. "Cut it off at the head," Damien had said. That had to be a clue!

Her fingers hovered over top of the keyboard.

Spark AI.

Luminous Data.

Just another big tech company, from the webpage she was skimming. Duh. She should have remembered. She certainly had heard about them on the coding forums. Some people questioned what they were doing. Specifically, the company's ethics, as far as she could remember. When did the industry motto "Don't be evil" disappear?

Or was it only ever a joke?

Cut it off at the head.

The head.

The lead part of the software code? Isabella's fingers drummed on the space bar.

"Who's the head of the company that makes Spark AI?" Robin asked.

Of course.

The CEO!

The head of the snake!

Was Damien Crowe going to attempt an assassination?

Isabella did more searching. This proved to be trickier. Since the company hadn't gone public nor was traded on the stock markets, corporate information about them was buried. Well hidden. But she dug around and soon enough found a name.

Bruce Bena.

Isabella opened another window and searched for anything she could find about him. She had to sort through three other Bruce Benas in the Western world. But she was pretty sure it wasn't the Bruce Bena who worked at a flower shop out in Montana, and likely not the other one who was a DJ and still lived in his parents' basement.

No, if Luminous Data was a local company, then in all likelihood so was the correct Bruce Bena.

Another search. More digging.

There he was!

She had him.

Bruce's home address. In a wealthy district on the outskirts of the city. Plus his cell number. Birthdate. College transcript. All the standard government-issued essentials.

Isabella flipped open another VPN window, allowing her to hide her own computer's identity. By now, she was five levels deep with encryption. Like wearing a full face mask over top of another one and so on. She ducked into the back end of the Department of Motor Vehicles.

A speeding ticket. For going fifty-four in a twenty-five zone. Three years ago. Paid. Plus several unpaid parking violations.

Bruce Bena drove a high-end Mercedes. Swapped it out every year for the latest model.

A registration for a boat.

No, a yacht. A sixty-four-footer.

Clearly Luminous Data was making money. Or at least Bruce was, as the CEO of the company.

He also had a handful of condos in the tropics.

Plus offshore bank accounts.

"Where is he now?" Anika asked. "Is he at work? Can you even tell?"

"Can I tell where he is?" Isabella asked, a bit surprised. "Clearly you guys don't understand what information about yourself is out there on the Internet, being bought and sold," she said, opening new portals into the back ends of Verizon, AT&T, and T-Mobile. "Even if our Bruce Bena has a specially designed phone with extra built-in security, I can still tell you the last thing he added to his grocery list. If he watches Netflix or Amazon Prime. I can even go through his calendar and rearrange his appointments."

That statement had the desired effect.

A hush fell over the group.

Isabella stood up.

Her fingers never stopped moving. Typing. As with one hand, she lifted the laptop from the desk in the middle of the grocery store.

She wandered over toward the faded sign that read DELI.

"Chad, will you open it up?" she asked.

With a nod, Chad pulled back the rusty folding curtain, revealing—

The Sneaky Inc. food truck!

Still half-painted, but when they weren't busy with the problem at hand, the team would finish it. Isabella promised herself!

Isabella's typing hand only paused long enough to open the

back door on the food truck. She climbed in. Grabbing a few pieces of equipment from off the wall racks, she collected just what she needed. With the flick of a switch, the main bank of computer monitors inside the truck powered on.

Isabella set down her laptop and began plugging the first of the gray boxes into it. One after another, she daisy-chained the various electronics together. A Raspberry Pi. A handful of Libre Computer boards. An Odroid-N2+. All working in harmony. Providing level after level of multi-processing.

Allowing Isabella to go deeper.

Faster.

Uncovering more and more of Bruce Bena's personal life.

Oddly enough, his phone was off right now.

Why was that?

Was he at the gym?

Did she dare turn it back on? Remotely?

Not yet.

Isabella pushed deeper.

Into Luminous Data's business email client.

The shared corporate calendar system.

Bruce was labeled "Out of Office."

That wasn't good enough.

Where was the man exactly?

Was he in hiding?

Tiny LED lights blinked all around her. The computer hardware working at full speed. Cooling fans whirling.

And then Isabella found something.

In the man's personal calendar.

A single entry.

Hold up. Was this going too far? Had she herself pushed past what was ethical ? Way past?

All to help save the man?!

The group all stood around her. Complicit.

Silently reading the single entry that read:

"Gallbladder Operation."

41

"We're gonna suit up on the way to the hospital!" Robin hollered, yanking off his sneakers. Thankfully, he had brought his new boots with him.

He glanced down at his watch.

Forty-nine minutes remaining.

When Damien gave his ultimatum, Robin had set a timer.

And they were losing time.

Fast!

Robin slipped on his boots again—

Only to feel it.

Just as his foot pressed into the sole of the boot. His sock made a squishing sound.

"NO!" he yelled. "Why God, why?! Did I offend you or something? Did I break some holy law that now my new boots can't go without being destroyed?!"

Chad shot him a concerned look. But it didn't last. Chad moved past too quickly, busy collecting his own last-minute items.

Robin frowned and laced up his boots. He probably shouldn't

have said what he did, but right then, he didn't care. He wanted to complain. It felt good. A chance to vent after all the little things that were not working for his own good!

He would just ignore it.

The cold, wet feeling in his one foot.

He would have to. The fate of one man was counting on it!

Robin plopped himself down into the driver's seat of the food truck. "Everyone ready?" he barked.

He got three thumbs-up in the rearview mirror.

And with that, he cranked the key.

The food truck engine groaned.

BRR, BRRR!

It rumbled and coughed a few times.

But it didn't start.

Everything inside of Robin wanted to explode.

But he didn't let it.

That wasn't what a leader did.

"God, help this engine to start," he whispered. "And I'm sorry that I just complained. Please forgive me."

Robin reached out for the truck key, cautiously this time—

Like it might bite him!—

And turned it again.

The engine roared to life!

"Thank you," Robin whispered, stifling a laugh. Was God really at work in the big *and* small things of life? He had to be!

Robin mashed the garage door opener clipped to the visor above his head.

And after the large delivery door lifted—

The Sneaky Inc. team pulled out!

Anika bent down and checked her tool belt again. Placing a hand on every object, she counted.

It was all there.

Each hand and cordless tool was present and accounted for.

Satisfied, she turned her attention back to Isabella. "So, help me understand this. Damien Crowe just stole a powerful weapon. And he's going to use it against the guy who made the AI Spark?"

"Yes," Isabella said. "But I don't think this is a typical weapon. I've been doing some reading. From what I understand, this isn't one that explodes or anything like that. I think it has to be an EMP. That stands for electromagnetic pulse."

Anika cinched her seatbelt tighter. "So, if it doesn't explode and hurt people—"

"It hurts electronics. Shuts them down. Not only will everything electronic in the area stop working, but it will also fry them dead."

"Then why doesn't Damien cut off the head by using the EMP weapon against the Spark AI computers instead of going after the CEO of the company? It doesn't make sense."

"Good question," Isabella replied. "I don't know. It might be that Damien is trying to make a bigger statement. To let all the other large tech companies making their own AI realize they should stop before he hunts them down next. I don't know."

Chad leaned forward, trying to get in on the conversation. "So, we're *not* after a bunch of Damien's thugs with big guns?"

Isabella shook her head. "I don't think so. I wish it were that easy. But you all heard him. Damien threatened that there would be collateral damage. Remember that part? I'm guessing Damien is planning something far worse than merely taking out Bruce Bena. He's threatening to take out the entire hospital. He could do it, too, now that he has the HIJENKS. Just imagine what that would do to a working hospital!"

"It would kill all the power inside," Anika said.

"Not only that . . ." Isabella said, her face turning white. She hesitated, unable to say more.

Chad filled in the silence. "It would do more than that. It would destroy the hospital's back-up generators. And all the machinery inside the place. Heart monitors. MRIs and X-ray machines. Including any devices providing oxygen to patients, keeping them alive."

Anika swallowed hard.

It was painting a picture in her head. An ugly one. And one just about as evil as they came. "Including the machines keeping Bruce Bena alive on the operating table!"

42

Thirty-two minutes remaining.

Robin didn't care if he was parking illegally. He rammed the brakes and threw the gearshift into park. Yes, right outside the hospital's emergency entrance!

From the corner of his eye, Robin spied a figure rapidly approaching.

"Hey, you can't park here!"

"Listen, buddy!" Robin growled, unbuckling his seat belt in a new record time. "You don't understand. This is an emergency! The entire hospital—"

He spun to address the medical staff person—

Only, it wasn't a hospital employee.

The looks of surprise on everyone's faces likely mirrored each other.

"Zeke?!"

"Robin?!"

Sure enough, the CIA was already on the scene. Several adults marched in and out of the hospital, while others set up barricades in front of the door. All of the agents wore navy blue jackets with the letters CIA emblazoned on the back in bright yellow.

Why hadn't the FBI ever issued *them* colored jackets?!

Robin shoved the thought aside.

"Zeke, does the CIA know about the assassination attempt on—!"

"Bruce Bena's life? Yes, of course," Zeke said with a smug look. "We know all about that." He took a step back and eyed the food truck. His face screwed up. "Is that standard-issue these days for the FBI?"

Robin couldn't answer.

Mia casually approached Robin's window. Standing next to her brother, she leaned into the truck, offering a wave to the others inside.

"But—but—" Robin fumbled his words. "Does the CIA know about—"

"Look, guys. I can appreciate that you want to help and all, but I'm pretty sure the CIA has everything under control." Zeke peered over his shoulder. "So why don't you move this hunk of junk to a regular parking spot and—well, hey, we'll call you if we need any snacks!" And with that, Zeke patted the hood of the food truck. He and Mia retreated toward the other CIA staff just outside the hospital doors.

Twenty-nine minutes.

Robin could not believe this!

They. Weren't. Needed!

He calmly adjusted the gearshift into reverse—

BEEP, BEEP.

And backed the truck up.

That had *not* gone according to plan.

The wind in his sails was gone.

Completely!

"Now what do we do?!" Chad croaked from the passenger's seat. "Sit back and watch the CIA do everything?!"

Robin shook his head. "I honestly don't know."

"And what if they botch it up?!" Isabella's voice growled from the back. "What if the CIA doesn't understand what's at stake?! Do they even know about the EMP?!"

Robin remained silent as he pulled the food truck into the back of the general lot and shoved it into park again.

For a moment they all just sat there.

The heavy silence nearly smothered them.

"Listen," Robin said, spinning around in his seat to face the team. He glanced at his watch and the ticking countdown. And despite all the things working against them, he had a sudden moment of peace. "I know this wasn't what was expected. What we had in mind. But we need to remember, nothing takes God by surprise. At least He knew this was coming. So, as much as I don't like it, we might need to sit this one out."

"Are you serious?!" Anika suddenly roared, her face getting red. "You're gonna just sit here and do nothing?! Unbelievable! And after *you* accused *me* of not contributing enough to the team?! Ha, that's rich coming from you, the quitter!"

Robin opened his mouth but didn't know what to say.

What Anika was saying did not compute.

When had he said that?

Anika didn't let up, jumping to her feet. She pointed an accusing finger in Robin's direction. "I'm sick and tired of all this! I'm trying my very best to work just as hard as everyone else. I do my part! And what? You don't even have the guts to tell me to my face that I'm not measuring up?! Or is this more than just you? Did the three of you all discuss this behind my back, huh?!"

Anika grabbed the back door and flung it open. "You know what?! I don't want to know. If none of you think what I'm doing is good enough, then I QUIT!"

Without waiting for any response, she marched out of the truck—

And was gone!

43

Anika heard the footsteps following after her.

But she didn't care.

She had said her piece—

And she was sticking to it!

"Anika, wait up!" Robin yelled from behind her.

Anika didn't stop. She didn't even slow down. And with the hot tears that now streamed down her face, she had absolutely no idea where she was going. Or how to get home from there.

Anika couldn't even bring herself to think about all the things she would miss. Their history. Bringing Marlin Ledger to justice. Saving the USA from a nuclear bomb together!

And now it was all over.

She had ripped off the ugly bandaid. Once and for all!

She had been brave enough to do it. To say what had been on her mind. How long had it been in there? Simmering toward explosion?!

However long it was, it was too long!

She wasn't interested in doing nothing. And she *most certainly* wasn't interested in doing Robin's work! Not anymore!

211

"Anika, will you hold up for a sec?!" Robin yelled, grabbing her arm.

That did it!

Anika yanked her arm clear of his grasp—

And cocking it back—

She swung at him!

What was she doing?!

Even Anika didn't know.

Only, Robin must very well have had a sense of what was coming. Because at the last second, he ducked.

Her punch barely missing him.

Unfortunately—

THWACK!

Her fist connected with something else.

"OWW!" Chad bellowed, clutching the side of his head. "You punched me in the EAR!"

"I am so, soooo sorry!!" Anika cried, trying to offer some sort of condolences to the writhing boy. "I wasn't trying to hit you! I was aiming for—"

Silence.

Her eyes connected with Robin's.

"Aiming for me," Robin whispered. His face looked concerned. Softened, somehow.

Anika looked away. The shame was too much. She didn't want to see Robin that way. She liked him better when he was hard and all business!

"Help me understand, Anika," Robin said quietly. "I'm sorry if I ever said something that might make you think you weren't wanted and needed on the team."

Anika spun back around.

Now that was more like it. Denial. At least that she could deal with! Not the mushy empathy thing or whatever that look had been.

"Your text message to me!" Anika growled, wiping away the tears and making a stand in the parking lot. "You honestly don't remember?! Here, look at this!" She held out her phone, displaying the text thread.

Gingerly taking the phone, Robin looked at it, with Isabella peering over his shoulder.

"Hello?" Chad said, righting himself again. "Does it concern anyone else that I can no longer hear from my one ear?!"

"I—I didn't write that," Robin said, shaking his head. He looked Anika square in the eyes. "I understand that it has my name and phone number attached . . . but I did *not* send that message."

"If you didn't send it, then who did?!"

Silence.

DING.

Another message suddenly appeared on Anika's screen.

It read:

> JK

Just kidding??
DING

> Zero Day!

Suddenly, Isabella got animated. "It's that hacker!" she blurted. "The one who sent all the people to our truck. All the cupcakes! They must have figured out how to get inside our phones. They're placing fake messages there to confuse us!"

Isabella turned to Robin. "Have you gotten any other weird texts?"

"I don't know," Robin said, pulling out his phone. He turned it on and was about to hand it over to the computer expert—

When he stopped.

His face washed completely white.

"What?" Isabella said. "Did you get one from me? Why, what did it say?!"

She reached for Robin's phone—

But he yanked it away.

As his face turned beet red.

"Um, no. Not really. I mean, maybe, but I don't—I don't think so." Robin fumbled with his phone, shoving it back into his pocket.

Isabella shared a knowing grin with Anika.

"HELLO!" Chad marched into the middle of the turmoil. "I can only hear mono now and have completely lost all sense of stereo. That doesn't concern anyone else?!"

44

Robin tried to relax.

Especially his face. It practically radiated heat!

He didn't want to smile or frown. He wanted everything to go back to the way it was only moments ago. A straight face. One that was under control. Before the completely and utterly embarrassing incident!

It was good to set things straight again. At least, with those on the team.

Who knew a hacker could seed such dissent among the group.

Confusing truth with lies!

And they would have to dig into this further. Stop the sophomoric jokes before they turned into something worse.

Sixteen minutes.

But now was *not* the time!

"Okay, Anika's right," Robin said, rallying the troops. "We can't sit back and do nothing if there's a chance the CIA doesn't have all the facts. If that's the case, they can't help but botch the mission. We'll be held responsible for not telling them everything we know!"

Marching back toward the food truck, Robin and the others grabbed their gear. The backpacks and utility belts that weren't already attached. And without hesitation, the team marched back to the emergency entrance.

To Zeke and Mia!

"How is Damien going to do it?" Robin quizzed the siblings, taking a stance before the sliding doors. "How is he going to assassinate a man that you have surrounded, huh? With enough guns this side of the Alamo all guarding him in the operating room. Tell me that?"

"He isn't," Mia said with confidence. "That's the point."

"But what about the HIJENKS weapon? What if Damien has it hidden somewhere on site, like he did with the Stingray device in the hotel? What then?"

Mia looked like she was going to respond.

Then didn't.

A look of concern came over Zeke's face.

Robin planted his hands on his hips. "Tell me, at the very least, that you've looked for it!"

Zeke yanked a walkie-talkie off his belt. Turning to the side, he whispered into the mouthpiece. "Um, has anyone considered an EMP attack on the hospital? Or what that might do to it?"

A crisp voice responded. "Negative."

"Hey, I think we started off on the wrong foot," Robin said, extending his hand. "Is there any way our two teams here could work together?"

"Let bygones be bygones!" Chad said loudly. Like he was talking with headphones on.

Mia looked at her brother.

And vice versa.

They shared a look of concern. Thinking.

"Alright," Zeke said finally, spinning back to shake Robin's hand. "But just this once, deal?"

"Deal!" Robin grinned. He glanced at his watch.

Fourteen minutes.

"But we better start working on a plan B," Robin said. "Just in case we don't find the HIJENKS in time."

Zeke nodded. "What do you have in mind?"

———

They split up.

Three teams.

Robin and Zeke raced through the hallways of the hospital.

But what exactly were they looking for?

Something the size of a torpedo. A missile shape, roughly five feet long and a foot wide.

Or had Damien pulled the guts of the weapon out? That would make the device so much smaller. Something that size could be hidden almost anywhere!

"This is hopeless!" Zeke yelled. "We're never going to find it!"

Robin stopped running.

He paused at an intersection, looking left and right.

Then he looked up to think.

"Help me process this," Robin said, drumming a thumb against his belt. "How would you smuggle in a HIJENKS device with no one thinking twice about it, huh?"

"I don't know. Maybe you'd disguise it first."

"Exactly," Robin said. "Then you could just roll the device inside and no one would ever question it."

"Like with the housekeeper's cleaning cart!" Zeke blurted.

The two boys took off again, scanning every nursing cart they came to!

———

Isabella and Anika jabbed at the button again.

The hospital elevator was taking forever!

And as soon as the door split open—

They both jumped inside.

"I'm sorry," Anika said to the male passenger, who was clutching a bouquet of flowers. "This is an emergency!"

The gentleman eyed the two girls.

One whose mascara streaked down her face.

The other who was full-on biting her nails.

He seemingly decided to take the next elevator and stepped out.

Isabella stabbed the button next to the words: Operating Room.

And the set of doors closed.

Silence.

Both of their eyes stared at the numbers above the elevator controls as they slowly descended.

Anika broke the silence. "Isn't everything inside the food truck gonna get fried if this thing goes off?"

Isabella shook her head. "Thankfully, no. With that much metal wrapped around it, the truck itself becomes a Faraday cage and should protect our tech."

"A Fara-*what*?"

Isabella turned her gaze to Anika and smirked. "Oh, I could really geek out right about now and explain it all, but—"

"But maybe now's not the time?"

"Precisely!"

DING.

The elevator doors slipped open.

The girls didn't hesitate.

With their badges raised, they sprinted off toward the entrance to the operating wing!

45

Squeezing the hand brake, Mia pulled her bright green and black Kawasaki Ninja motorcycle to a stop.

She yanked off her glossy black helmet—

Letting her glossy black hair fall down around her shoulders.

Out flipped the kickstand.

Leaning to one side, Mia slipped off her bike.

Except a figure remained sitting on the back.

Chad.

With an oversize helmet tilted over his head, his eyes were still clenched shut. His arms were outstretched in front of him, hugging nothing, apparently.

"Are we there yet?!" he yelled, cracking open one eye.

A large orange sign nearby read: HOME DEPOT.

"That had to be the most insane driving I have ever experienced!" Chad blurted. "And I thought *I* was a sketchy driver. Wow! I cannot believe we're still alive!"

Mia just shook her head.

Chad followed her into the big box store.

They didn't have time to waste. They both ran toward the aisle labeled "Generators."

Sure enough, the store had plenty of options to choose from.

But they all looked small.

"Hey, can you help us?" Mia grabbed a lady in an orange vest passing by. "We need a portable generator—and like, now!"

"Alrighty there," the stock worker said with a touch of Southern twang. "What size would you be lookin' for, sweetheart?"

"One big enough to run a hospital!" Chad shouted with a finger in his ear.

Several other shoppers turned to glare.

"Oh my!" the worker gasped. She led them a little ways down the aisle, pointing out a model. "This one would do well for that. Of course, you must mean *one room* of a hospital, surely."

"No." Chad shook his head. He leaned in closer in case he wasn't being heard. "We need one to run the *entire* hospital!"

"Heavens! We don't sell anything that big, I'm afraid," the worker said with a growing look of worry.

Mia put a hand on Chad's arm. "Let me handle this." She turned back to the employee. "I'm sorry, ma'am. But what's the largest model you do carry?"

The staff person walked a few more feet away, pointing at the latest model.

It was the size of a photocopier and wrapped in a neat plastic shell.

"It's the model for an entire house," she said. "But I'm afraid it isn't portable. It has to weigh nearly three hundred pounds. And I'm afraid it still isn't as big as you seem to think you need."

"That's alright, thanks." Mia waved to the worker, dragging Chad behind her. "We gotta look somewhere else!"

"Hold up, hold up," Chad said, dragging her to a stop near the

222

exit. With a finger still in his ear, he shook it, speaking as loudly as ever. "With my balance still off, I sure hope I don't have to climb back on that pocket rocket of yours!"

————

Nine minutes.

"Whoa!" Zeke exclaimed, yanking open the set of double cabinet doors on a cart and immediately stepping back.

"Wait, you found it?" Robin raced past a pair of nurses in order to see.

Sure, enough, there it was.

The double-wide cart wasn't even all that well disguised. It had a blood pressure collar on top of it, along with a computer monitor that wasn't plugged in.

Yet in the midst of a busy hospital, anyone could have easily overlooked it!

Inside sat the inner electronics of the HIJENKS weapon. The outer missile-shaped cone was gone. A small digital timer displayed the matching time from Robin's watch.

Eight minutes.

"What an idiot!" Zeke said. "We can just roll this thing out of here and that'll solve our—"

But Robin interrupted him with a hand raised.

He eyed the device closer.

And the thin cable extending from it.

Nearly hidden, the thin cable neatly followed alongside a regular power cable.

Robin traced them both.

All the way to an outlet where the thin cable was plugged in.

Shaking his head, he frowned.

"This thing is booby-trapped," Robin whispered. He followed

the thin cable back to the cart. The narrow wire appeared to feed into the bottom shelf.

As gingerly as possible, Robin tugged on the bottom set of doors.

KR-CLICK.

Without much effort, they both opened.

Revealing stack after stack of neatly organized bricks.

Of something that looked like gray putty.

The material covered the entire bottom of the cart.

And neatly printed on the clear cellophane that wrapped each brick were the same words:

C-4 EXPLOSIVE!

46

R obin leaned back.

"Um," Zeke whispered. A streak of glistening sweat slalomed down his face. "Do you know anything about defusing explosives?"

"A little," Robin grimaced, slipping out of his vest. Things were getting hot, and he didn't like it.

And he *especially* didn't like explosives. They were not as forgiving as he liked.

Zeke grabbed his walkie-talkie. "Control, we need to clear the entire building. And I mean, now!" His radio squawked with feedback. "We have enough explosives up here—" Zeke looked around and then added in a whisper—"to level the entire fourth floor!"

If Robin was going to deal with this latest problem, at least he could be comfortable doing it. He hunkered down, sitting on the floor. And felt the squish of his sock as he did so. That was definitely *not* helping!

"So, what do we have here?" Robin mused, gently guiding a

pencil through the detonators and the network of wires that fed them.

He traced the detonator cords back to their origin.

A circuit board.

It wasn't much bigger than three inches square. A computer chip of sorts. But it had about a thousand little metal leads criss-crossing over it. A nightmare of connections!

Despite all its complicated electronics, it was simple.

Unplug the cart and—

BOOM!

"Robin, we can't stay here!" Zeke breathed in his ear. "Forget it! We'll clear the hospital and—"

"There's no time," Robin said calmly. "Look around you. You think you can clear an entire hospital with half the people stuck in bed?"

Six minutes.

Zeke's face lost color.

The walkie-talkie shook in his hand. He clutched it with both hands, probably trying to stop himself from shaking.

"No, it won't work." Zeke could barely get the words out. "We have to go, Robin. We have to leave!"

But Robin shook his head. With his vest laid out on the floor beside him, he slipped a pair of wire cutters from one of its pockets.

"I'm not leaving."

———

Anika held out her leather wallet, clearly displaying her FBI credentials.

The CIA agent guarding the operating room squinted.

Then he leaned back. "I'm sorry, I can't let you in. I need confirmation from my superiors before letting anyone inside."

"But you don't understand!" Isabella growled, stepping forward. "There is a very real possibility this entire hospital is about to be plunged into complete darkness! Including every device that is keeping that man inside there alive!"

The CIA serviceman didn't flinch.

If anything, he gripped the M16 rifle in front of him tighter.

"If the surgeons don't stop what they are doing," Anika yelled, "Bruce Bena is a dead man!"

"I'm sorry, I have my orders." The other agent was losing his cool. "Now I must insist that you leave or I will have you escorted out!"

———

"Hold on just a minute!" Mia spat in Chad's face. "I thought you had me pull into the Burger King drive-through because you had *an idea*!"

"I do," Chad said equally loudly, but with none of the passion. He grabbed another clump of French fries and shoved them into his mouth. "But I think better on a full stomach. Want some?" He held out the fry container.

"Unbelievable!" Mia blurted, throwing up both arms. "Does your entire team think you're as *completely* insane as I do?!"

Chad stopped chewing, his face suddenly serious. "Is that a trick question?"

Mia buried her face in both hands.

Just as an oversize pickup truck pulled into the drive-through beside them at the outdoor seating area.

A monster truck! With large knobby wheels and a lifted

227

suspension. In addition to a large American flag, it flew another smaller flag that read "Best in Show."

Chad eyed it—

And stopped chewing.

"Aren't cars and most vehicles essentially a rolling generator?" he asked.

Mia stared at Chad.

Then at the obnoxious vehicle.

Was this simply more of the boy's madness?!

"I don't know," Mia said. "Is that important right now? What are you getting at?!"

Tilting his head back, Chad poured the last of the fries into his open mouth. At best, getting half in, half down his shirt.

Chewing like a cow, Chad spoke after a big swallow.

"Ever been to a car show?"

47

The CIA had cleared many of the floors of their medical staff and patients.

The last of the occupied hospital beds were being quickly wheeled past.

It was too much!

There were too many wires.

And all the same color!

Robin wiped his brow. There was no way to know which wire to cut. It was a jumble of madness. Pure chaos!

And if he tampered with the HIJENKS weapon itself—

A tilt sensor he had found would trigger it. Activating the EMP!

3:00

2:59

2:58

Maybe Zeke was right.

Maybe the best they could do was get out of there.

Leave and let the chips fall where they may. Except in this case, it would be chunks of the hospital falling where they may!

Robin started to get up to leave—

When it came to him.

A download of understanding!

The explosives circuit board. Robin only needed to short it in order to temporarily deactivate it. He saw it in his mind. Like a 3D model rotating before him. Damien might be a brilliant mastermind, but he had forgotten to build his creation with a limiter.

Instead, he'd used a cheap circuit!

"Zeke!" Robin exclaimed. A new surge of hope coursed through him. "Find me a wet rag! I don't know, a piece of gauze run under the faucet. Something!"

For a moment, Zeke froze. He looked around him and appeared overcome with cabinets and drawers and all sorts of medical storage devices!

Robin jumped to his feet to help.

Drawer after drawer was flung open.

Cabinets yanked wide!

Both boys shoveled through an endless amount of supplies.

Surgical masks, blood pressure monitors, and boxes of pregnancy test strips.

They had all the urine sample jars, rubber crutch pads, and digital thermometers they could want!

"How can we be inside a hospital," Zeke yelled from sheer frustration, "and not find a single gauze pad?!"

Blood bags. Rubber gloves. Even a box of last year's candy canes!

Not a single rag!

1:10

1:09

1:08

Until Robin lunched for the next cabinet and heard it—

SQUISH.

It was quiet. Almost imperceptible. It was more likely he had felt it and only imagined that he heard it. But that didn't stop him.

Robin dropped and immediately yanked off his bootlaces!

He shook his head. A part of him couldn't believe this was going to solve his problem. Not for real, could it?!

"AAAGH!" Robin screamed, tugging on his boot, which didn't want to come off. He tugged harder. The boot popped off and, abandoning it, he scrambled for his damp sock.

SLURP.

And pulled it off!

"But my God shall supply all your needs according to his riches in glory by Christ Jesus!" Robin laughed and folded his sock over a few times. He wanted the bottom part. The section that was the soggiest!

:37

:36

:35

Robin cringed as he held the folded sock over the circuit board.

"Wait!" Zeke hissed. "You're not actually going to use your dirty, smelly sock to—"

:29

:28

But Robin was.

And he did!

As he foolishly shielded his face and—

Mashed his damp sock into the circuit board.

FZZZZ, SIZZLE, CRACKLE!

It sputtered and sparked.

Did it work?!

There was only one way to really tell!

Robin reached for the power cord and pulled on it—

THUNK.

Unplugged it.

Nothing.

Robin opened one eye.

Then let out a whoop!

:19

:18

Robin jumped to his feet. He had stopped the explosives that prevented them from moving the cart, but there was still the HIJENKS weapon. Using both hands, he pushed on the cart.

Slow and steady!

The EMP was still wired to a tilt sensor. He would have to do this very carefully!

The wheels squeaked straight toward the window.

Now if only Robin could lift the window open.

Or break it!

Zeke ran up from behind him. "We're running out of time!"

Without warning, he grabbed the cart from Robin—

And raced forward with it.

"No, Zeke! Stop! It has a tilt sensor insi—"

Robin never finished his sentence. Not before—

ZORRRN!!!

Every medical device around them sparked. Exploded!

There was an intense flash of light. Pops and bangs!

As electronics overloaded.

Cooking themselves with an overabundance of power.

Just before the entire hospital—

Plunged into darkness!

48

Around the corner from the CIA guards, Isabella slapped a piece of paper against the large glass window looking into the operating room. She and Anika hadn't had time to make it neat.

On the other side of the paper were three giant scrawled letters.

S.O.S.

And while Isabella held the paper in place for all the medical workers inside the OR to see, Anika pounded on the glass.

Several of the nurses and at least one doctor looked up.

One even pointed to the sign.

Clearly there was conversation inside about it. Isabella could see their masks moving but she couldn't read any lips.

There were looks of concern.

And work over the blue tissue paper–covered patient momentarily stopped.

Anika waved a nurse to approach the glass.

The nurse hesitated. Then neared.

The woman had red eyebrows, her hair entirely bound up in a

surgeon's cap. As she approached the glass, she lowered her face mask and opened her mouth, just when—

ZORRRN!!!

A flash of light! Sparks and small explosions erupted from the banks of electronics that surrounded the medical staff!

Anika slapped her hand against the glass, trying to reach out—

As darkness separated everyone!

———

While Chad picked at a cone of cotton candy, Mia looked around her.

This was most definitely a car show.

And then some!

There had to be the biggest and most grotesque vehicles here that she had ever seen. Lifted pickups. Monster trucks. Neon-colored semitruck cabs that belched flames out of their upward-pointing exhaust pipes. Even one truck that was dwarfed by its own tires!

Mia couldn't help but laugh.

This was silly. A circus of metal and chrome!

Who would actually paint their trucks this way? Or make them so tall that you needed an extra ladder just to climb inside them?!

Chad tugged on Mia's sleeve.

She could just make out what he was saying over the roaring of the surrounding engines.

"In case you're wondering," Chad yelled, "I have two pieces of good news. Number one: I think my hearing has finally come back. That had me worried there for a time. I thought I was going to have to learn sign language."

Chad shoved another large wad of cotton candy into his mouth.

"What is the second thing?!" Mia shouted over the noise of the crowd. "Or don't I want to know?!"

"I found an electrical generator big enough. And believe it or not, it's mobile!"

"Really?!" Mia said, looking around them. "Where?!"

But when Chad pointed, it wasn't as close as Mia had imagined.

Nor the size she had pictured.

Because what Chad pointed to was a dump truck.

On display in the center of the dirt track.

Only, this was no ordinary dump truck.

Unless Mia and Chad had shrunk, this thing was beyond imagination.

For the centerpiece at the car show was none other than—

A deep-mining dump truck!

It easily towered over everything else near it.

Including the grandstands.

Even the lights illuminating the track!

It had to be two or three times as wide as its closest competitor!

There was no way Mia could even jump up and touch the wheel wells.

And a person wouldn't need an extra ladder to climb into one of these behemoths.

Because this one had a staircase permanently welded to the front of it!

Chad sat behind the steering wheel of the world's largest vehicle. A mining dump truck capable of holding over four hundred and fifty tons of rubble!

All comfortable and settled in.

With the classic rock channel playing.

Almost like he had done this before!

CRUNCH!

Chad leaned out his open window and yelled, "Sorry! My bad!"

As he flattened another parked car.

How had Mia gotten to this point?

Where a small kid who looked like he might be nine years old, with bent ears that made him sorta resemble one of Santa's elves, had sauntered up to the center-stage vehicle at the local car show and helped himself up into the cab?!

The same kid who hot-wired the ignition and justified it all by saying he was only "borrowing" the dump truck.

"Look out!" Mia screamed.

CRASH!

Too late.

The herculean dump truck squashed another parked car. A Jaguar F-Type. Expensive!

Oh, and an entire bus stop!

Thankfully both were empty!

BRRT, BRRT!

The Jaguar's alarm continued to sound despite the luxury car only being inches thick now!

The dump truck took up every lane. Hurtling down the city streets! With people diving away for their lives!

Another row of parked cars approached. Mia braced. One arm shot out, stabilizing herself against the dash.

"You know," Chad said, raising his motorized seat another

inch, "it really does have a rather comfortable ride, all things considered. Good shock absorbers, a decent sound system. They only thing missing really, other than a rearview mirror—"

CRUNCH, CRASH, SPLAT!

"Is a pair of fuzzy dice!"

49

Robin's stomach dropped.

He couldn't believe what had just happened.

It was surreal. Dreamlike.

And very eerie.

The darkened hospital hallways.

The only light came in from the windows.

Even the exit signs were no longer offering anything.

But it was the sounds, or lack thereof, that haunted him the most.

A profound silence rarely heard in such an environment.

No hum of machinery.

No buzz of the heating/cooling vents.

No blips or beeps from monitors.

Photocopiers and computer fans sat motionless.

No ringing of phones.

All the background noises that he had so often taken for granted—

Instantly gone!

"I'm—I'm sorry," came a whisper.

It was Zeke.

He was silhouetted up ahead. Robin couldn't see the expression on his face. Only, he heard it in the waver of his voice. A sorrow—a humility—that hadn't been there before.

"I thought we were out of time," Zeke lamented. "I'm sorry. I didn't know that it would detonate early. Honestly, I just—"

"Listen," Robin interrupted. "Don't worry about it now. If it hadn't happened to you, it could have happened to me. What we need to do is—"

And that's when Robin heard it.

Zeke must have as well, since he turned his head to listen.

A new sound.

A deep, groaning sound.

Like thunder, but as if the storm were still far away.

What was it?!

Robin and Zeke abandoned the cart, moving instead to the window at the end of the hallway. The closer they got to it, the louder the sound.

A deep-throated rumble.

Punctuated occasionally with a high-pitched splash, almost.

The sun hung low in the sky.

Robin and Zeke each used a hand to shield the bright light from their eyes.

The window presented an outside view of one of the neighboring construction sites.

A thirty-story building towered above them. Little more than half complete. One side of the tower glittered with floor-to-ceiling mirrored windows. The other side was open, wrapped in orange thermal blankets to keep the wind away from the workers. It was little more than the skeletal bones of a future skyscraper. A sign hung about halfway up, flapping in the breeze.

It read OFFICES FOR RENT, then gave a phone number.

Were the noises really coming from the construction site?

The tower itself?

But how?

And why? Unless—

SPISH!

A full-sized bank of windows on the third floor of the tower suddenly exploded outward!

Glass shards twinkled in the light—

And rained to the ground below.

What was happening? Why did the glass break? Robin narrowed his eyes. A random window on a neighboring building merely decided to burst? Out of the blue?!

SPISH! SPISHH!

Two more large windows shattered!

One on the second story.

The other on the fourth floor.

"We better get out of here," Zeke whispered.

"I think you're right," Robin said, taking a step back. "Grab the cart in case we need it," he barked, his voice intensifying. "We need to get outside and see just how far that EMP strike might have affected things!"

———

Bathed in darkness, Isabella and Anika yanked out their phones at the same time.

And went to flick on the flashlight apps—

Only, Isabella's phone wouldn't turn on.

Neither would Anika's.

Isabella poked the screen again and again.

Neither of their electronic devices did anything. Bricked!

They could hear yelling from inside the operating room.

But there was nothing they could do.

Not now.

The only thing Isabella could strategize on was getting some light down there. She could hardly see enough to take the next step!

"The window," she whispered. She wasn't sure why she was being quiet at a time like this. Except it felt strange to be talking when all the sounds that had just been around them were now gone. "Find your way over to the window!"

With their hands outstretched, Isabella and Anika shuffled ahead, making slow progress.

"OW!" Anika growled. "I just kicked something!"

"What was it?"

"I don't know. I think it was a box of metal surgery pans," Anika whispered.

"Grab it! Anything reflective, pick up and carry!"

There were cries and screams coming out of the darkness. More medical staff confused by the power outage. More so because the generator back-up system clearly was no longer operational as well.

Isabella collected a shiny metal tray.

Anika had a metal bowl under one arm and a metallic bedpan in the other. Thankfully, it looked clean!

But eventually, threading past the CIA guard and the stranded medical staff, the girls arrived at the window.

"Hold up the objects," Isabella said. "In the little sunlight there is left."

And they did. It took a bit before they could bounce the light correctly. But once they got the hang of it, Isabella and Anika sent a bright shaft of light down the hallway, bringing some much-needed illumination to those stumbling around in the dark!

50

obin was the first to hit the street outside.

Pushing the cart, Zeke followed. But he lingered behind.

Robin half jogged, half ran toward the neighboring construction site.

The deep groaning noise was much louder here.

Sonorous.

And vibrated through the ground.

He could feel it through his new boots. Especially the foot that no longer had a sock.

It almost felt like an earthquake.

Or maybe the start of one.

The vibrations came and went. Moments of intensity. Then nothing.

Robin approached the tower construction, mostly looking upward. Careful to avoid any glass that still rained down.

Did he dare go closer?

Robin had to know what was happening if he was going to fix it.

"Lord, please be with me and guide me," he prayed. "Let me not go another step without me fully relying on you!"

It was a simple prayer. But it felt good to say. And it felt even better to believe in the one it was to!

Just then, as Robin took his next step—

He completely lost his footing, lunging forward!

It had looked like a flat concrete walkway.

Except it was anything but.

Wet cement!

Robin had marched right into it.

He couldn't believe it. First his one foot had squished down. Then, to keep his balance, he had foolishly used the other foot to keep from falling.

Now both feet were submerged. At least a foot deep!

And maybe worse yet, he was slowly sinking!

Robin pulled and tugged on his legs!

But they wouldn't budge. Not even an inch!

The thick, wet cement held him fast.

He yanked his knees upward again, trying harder this time.

But despite being red in the face and losing his breath—

All his efforts led to nothing.

He was stuck.

Stuck fast!

————

Mia wanted to close her eyes.

But she didn't dare!

She wasn't enjoying any part of this ride!

Give her a fast motorcycle any day.

This thing felt like driving a house!

And Chad was like a child on a go-cart track, weaving this way and that.

Hold on. He wasn't actually going out of his way to flatten parked cars, was he?!

But her attention was distracted by the seven-story hospital that suddenly came into view.

It looked eerily silent.

And from top to bottom, it was completely dark.

The EMP must have gone off. The event they dreaded had clearly happened!

Oh, they needed to hurry!

"AHHH!"

But that wasn't what took her breath away.

The best she could do was point.

At the incredibly tall building under construction that sat next to the hospital.

She couldn't be sure.

But from where she was sitting—

In the passenger's seat of an incredibly huge mining dump truck—

It appeared as though the EMP might have affected the skyscraper as well.

Because the thirty-story tower—

Was now leaning.

Ever so subtly—

Toward the hospital!

51

olding a reflective light, Anika helped direct people out of the hospital.

With none of the elevators working, the exits to the stairways had become blocked.

Overcrowded!

"One at a time!" she yelled. "No pushing!"

In their panic, people were acting like rowdy children.

All impatient to escape!

Anika shook her head.

Always babysitting!

———

Robin just stood there. Frozen in place.

He had put everything he had into pulling his feet out of the mire. But to no effect. If anything, all his struggling had only made him sink further!

But the pause gave him a chance to look inside the first floor of the construction. The source of the deep-throated groaning.

Robin leaned to one side, trying to get a better view. Why were the mechanical floor jacks bent like that? Weren't they holding up the next floor?

The entire building?!

No.

Robin felt a sinking feeling in his gut. The floor jacks were operated by electricity. It really would only take one to fail before it put more pressure on the next one.

And that in turn would domino into more and more failures.

And without the electrical backups—

It could spiral out of control.

SPISH!

Another window from somewhere above Robin gave way.

The immense pressures of a buckling infrastructure were having their effects.

KA-SINK! SINK! SINK!!

Large shards of glass rained down around Robin!

Piercing the wet cement!

He cowered, arm above his head.

Knife edges slamming all around him!

KA-SINK! SINK! SINK!!

When it finally stopped.

Robin opened an eye. His arms slowly slipping off his head.

He looked around him.

At the deadly glass spikes that jutted up from the wet cement.

And he hadn't been touched?

Robin quickly surveyed himself.

Seriously? Not even a single cut?!

GROOOOAAN!!

A new sound occurred. It was deep and vibrated the whole earth before him. Little ripples appeared in the surface of the wet cement.

The intense pressure caused several additional floor jacks to explode. Rocketing out from their position under the first floor—

KR-THUNK! KR-THUNK-THUNK!

The metal jacks sank into the side of a concrete mixer truck.

"Oh boy."

SPISH! SPISH!

With a renewed energy, Robin yanked on his legs.

Fortunately, the new glass fell to the side. But how long would that last?!

Breathing heavily, Robin stopped again.

He knew exactly what he could do.

What he *had* to do!

But he didn't want to do it.

"Oh, Lord. Why, oh why? Don't you understand that they're new boots?" Robin whispered, looking up and crying out to the heavens. "The best pair I've ever owned. And you're asking me to give them up! Why?!"

And then he saw it.

On the tenth floor or so.

A forklift—

Hung by a thin cable—

Teetering over the edge above him.

Robin didn't hesitate.

Pulling out a knife, he leaned over. Digging through the muck, he cut his laces. Or what he hoped were his laces and not his feet, since he couldn't see all that clearly!

KR-THUNK!

A crate of nails must have fallen from high above and burst open. Not twenty feet away!

KR-CRASH!

Then sheets of drywall arrived. Exploded on the ground in a cloud of dust and debris.

Robin sawed his knife faster.

Back and forth!

The best he could through the thick cement!

There!

He was through. And just when he heard a whistling sound approach—

Robin didn't look.

He dove.

Backward.

Abandoning his beloved pair of expensive, hand-stitched, supple, leather boots! Just as—

KR-BLAMMM!!!

The forklift obliterated the area where he had just been.

Sending a thick wave of wet cement in every direction.

Silence.

Robin wiped his face clear.

Barely able to see through the muck. Only enough to spy what remained of the destroyed vehicle—

One of the thick metal forks—

Buried deep in the asphalt and dirt.

Only an inch away!

52

Despite the equipment rolling off the slanting floors above, Robin couldn't get away quickly.

With his precious boots gone, he had one sock and a bare foot to proceed with.

While nails and shattered glass littered the ground!

Robin tiptoed forward, trying to find the bare spots.

But they were sparse!

"Ow, ow, ow!"

KR-SMASH! BANG!

And getting sparser. There was no way forward without destroying his feet.

He took another step.

The edges of broken glass cut deep!

"No, God. Please!"

And that's when he saw them.

Bright yellow boots.

They were nothing except hideous. Like a pair of oversize children's rain boots. They sat nestled beside a large spool of Romex cabling.

He wasn't going to put them on. No! He didn't care what happened. There simply was no way he would slip on a pair of ugly yellow—

CRANGG!

An industrial staple gun bounced off the ground and twisted in its rebound beside him—

Along with about a billion metal staples.

Robin frowned.

And changed his direction toward the boots.

A thin path seemed to present itself—

Straight to them.

And when they were just within reach—

Robin leaned forward, grabbing them!

"I don't mean to complain, God," he grumbled, climbing into the silly things. They were taller than he first thought, coming up to his hips. "But bright yellow? Seriously?!"

————

Even before Chad stopped the dump truck, Mia raced down the machine's front staircase. She took two steps at a time.

They were at the hospital's side entrance. Pulled up over the curb, several handicap parking spaces, and at least one commissioned decorative art piece.

This was the spot they had agreed on. Thankfully in advance of their comms going down.

The closest location to the hospital's back-up generator and within reach of its cables.

And as Mia's feet hit the sidewalk, she saw her brother dragging one of those thick cables toward her. It looked substantial. Nearly half as thick as a firefighter's hose.

Isabella and Anika burst through the side entrance door,

meeting them.

Chad left the dump truck running. He slid down the handrails and began working the inverter unit positioned between the back wheels. Tugging and pulling, Chad produced a similar-size cable, dragging it over his shoulder toward Zeke.

"Do it now! There's no time to second-guess this!" Isabella exclaimed. "They have Bruce Bena opened up on the operating table right now. And he's not going to last!"

"If we don't get that electricity back on," Anika said, "he's going to bleed out."

Robin approached.

Doing a strange sort of waddle with his goofy, oversize boots.

"I need to caution whoever plugs these together," Chad said, breathing heavily. He paused and gently set his cable down on the ground about six feet away from Zeke's. "There is enough power running through these cables to light up most of this building. Get them any closer and the electricity could arc between them. I can't express enough just how unfriendly that would be to the human body. Especially if they are not properly grounded."

That gave everyone pause.

Turning their eyes to the sidewalk.

To the two ends of the thick power cables.

And the potential for destruction they held.

———

You can do this, for I will be with you.

Robin heard the words.

He just wasn't completely sure he believed them.

Still, Robin broke the silence. "Zeke, your gloves." Robin motioned for them.

Zeke yanked off a set of large rubber gloves he must have found back with the generator.

Robin didn't hesitate. Shoving his hands into them, he reached down and grabbed Zeke's end of the cable.

There were people inside. People who were suffering.

Who would die if they weren't helped.

Robin leaned over, reaching for Chad's abandoned cable.

KR-SIZZLE!!

A blinding arc of electricity and light crackled between the two ends.

Everyone jumped!

The appearance of such power startled Robin himself.

But he didn't stop. Instead, he fought the fear!

CRACKLE, SNAP!!

The bolt of lightning between the two ends only intensified as they neared each other.

Even with his eyes fully shut, it was too bright.

Blinding.

But Robin pushed harder, shoving the two ends closer, just until—

CLICK.

They snapped together.

The light gone in a blink.

As the hospital itself lit up.

Floor after floor blinked back to life!

Robin set the cable down like it was fragile.

And backed away.

One problem down.

Now to solve the last one—

Before it *fell over*!

53

Robin and Chad ran toward the construction site.

The mighty tower was leaning at an even greater angle than before!

"How do you want to right it?" Chad yelled over the din of bending metal.

Robin paused next to the nurse cart Zeke had pushed out of the building. He peered inside at the HIJENKS device. It had triggered once already. Would it have the energy to trigger again? He couldn't worry about that.

His worry was more about his damp sock.

And if it had dried out too much already.

But with a cursory examination, it still looked like it was doing its job.

"I want to break the building's back," Robin explained, pushing the cart closer to the construction site. "The higher the better. If we can sever the support beams at the far side of the lean, the upper half should buckle backward, fall in on itself."

"You mean like hitting the backs of someone's knees at the same time?"

"Precisely!" Robin yelled. But the cart was now bumping over debris and jostling about. "This isn't going to work. Help me carry this!"

Skirting around the side of the leaning tower, Robin and Chad carried the heavy cart. Even after clearing off all the fake supplies, the explosives themselves proved to be quite a load.

They struggled with the cart, lugging it into the ground floor of the skyscraper.

The ground closest to the hospital looked like a war zone. With cinder blocks and other supplies crumbling, grinding to dust as they landed.

Most of the glass on that side of the building was now gone. Only the jagged edges remained.

The groan of the metal support beams seemed unbearable. Loud and piercing. Such a deep and thunderous noise that Robin felt it vibrating his insides!

But they wrestled the cart up the first set of concrete steps.

And then another.

It wasn't easy. Large cracks had formed in the cement. Chasms that widened every second!

Chad's face was bright red. He grunted and groaned. "I'm not sure . . . how much more . . . I can carry!"

Robin didn't respond. He couldn't. Not with his own muscles screaming at him! With sweat stinging his eyes!

Could they make it one more flight up?!

When their load suddenly got lighter.

As more hands came under the cart.

Zeke and Mia joined in!

Maybe the CIA wasn't so bad after all.

With the extra help, they moved double-time!

Up another flight of steps they wrestled the cart. They lugged it to the far side of the lean. Using a long power cord, Zeke lashed the cart to the support beam closest to the edge.

"Alright!" Mia yelled. "Now how do we set this off after we get out of here?!"

It was a good question.

One that Robin hadn't had the chance to think about until now.

And they had no time to ponder it!

Robin's eyes surveyed a nearby workbench. All the tools had slid into a pile at one end.

A chalk line.

It would have to do!

While the others completed strapping the cart into place, Robin unspooled the chalk line. It was a small container of chalk and string. Useful for making straight lines on construction sites. But not today. With the line fully extended, Robin connected the clip to the end of his wet sock. He did it as gingerly as possible, careful not to bump it. He wrapped the other end around his waist.

This was a deadman's job.

But one that someone had to do.

How far would he make it down the stairs?

One flight?

Maybe two?

He would never be far enough away before the C-4 triggered.

Not unless he jumped off the side of the building.

And then what?

God would just catch him?!

To his surprise, Chad seemed to have the same idea. Peering over the edge of the building, he backed up to get a good running start. "Cowabunga!" Chad yelled, and then with a complete leap of faith, the kid flung himself out into the great nothing.

And disappeared from sight.

Where did he go?

Robin knew Chad wasn't completely crazy. Well, he wasn't so sure about that. But why jump from the fourth-story ledge—

Unless there was a chance of safety?

No matter how slim!

Then Zeke and Mia took the same plunge off the side.

Did they too see something Robin couldn't see?!

CREEEAAAK!

The tower made a horrible sound!

It shook and bent even more.

No time.

This was faith!

Robin calmed himself, drying his sweaty palms on his pants.

Then he ran, and with everything he had left—

Leaped!

54

With a construction company using as much concrete as this one did, they mixed the stuff on-site. Which required one part cement and two parts sand.

That meant lots and lots of sand.

A massive mound of the stuff!

CLIP.

Weightless, Robin felt his chalk line grow taut—

Then snap free.

KA-BOOOOMMM!!!

Robin felt the heat before he saw it.

As a ball of explosion and flame sped toward him.

But before it could envelop him—

He dropped below it, landing—

TOOOF!

Onto the outer slope of the tall sand mound, which rose at least twenty feet tall. His ugly yellow boots almost were wide enough to allow Robin to surf down it. With a somersault at the end and sand all through his face and hair, he was back up on his feet again, on solid ground. Running!

As the mighty office tower behind him buckled in on itself.

Almost as if in slow motion.

Without its rear support beams, the upper portion of the building righted itself again. And then, with that much momentum, continued the other way. The bottom of the building collapsed into itself, sending the top half into the river. The whole thing eventually—

ROOARRR!

Crumbling into a pile of twisted metal and concrete!

And it was only after the massive dust cloud that enveloped everyone and everything for nearly a quarter mile settled—

That the teams could see the hospital again.

Unharmed—

And still standing strong!

———

Robin and the team were exhausted.

They all sat inside the familiar empty grocery store. Like statues. Like the wounded on a battlefield, trying to figure out if they were still alive—

Or dead.

Silence.

Damien Crowe hadn't been captured. Not yet, at least. But the FBI, by working alongside the CIA, had stopped him.

The life of Luminous Data's CEO, Bruce Bena, had been saved. He lost a lot of blood in the ordeal, but with the electrical power restored, the hospital staff pulled him back from the grave.

And then there were the countless others who had successfully returned to the hospital. The most critical patients first.

It could have been much worse.

Only, Robin didn't want to move.

Every muscle hurt.

And as much as he disliked the bright yellow boots that he still wore, he had no energy left to remove them.

As agonizing as it was, he lifted one leg, allowing a stream of sand to spill out from the upper edge.

"Good call on the boots," Chad said flatly, without his usual overabundance of energy. "You know you'd be a dead man if you hadn't changed 'em."

That got Robin's attention. He let the sand drain from the other one. Quite a little beach lay on the floor before him. "What do you mean?"

"Those boots." Chad motioned with his head. "They aren't cheap, you know. They're specially designed."

"What? These ugly yellow—" Robin crinkled his nose, not sure how to finish qualifying the things.

"Wait, I thought you knew," Chad said, sitting up. "Those are electrician's boots. There is *no* way you could have plugged those cables together and actually survived without wearing those. You did know that, right?"

"Um . . ."

That got everyone else's attention.

"Hold up," Anika chimed in. "You swapped your new boots out for those and you didn't even know what you were doing?!"

Robin went to say something.

But in the end, he didn't have anything to add.

He figured maybe he should just shut his mouth for once.

Before he did something stupid, like complain—

Or stick his foot in his mouth again!

55

A few days later, after some much-needed rest, Robin was out skateboarding again.

He wasn't going anywhere in particular.

Just out for a ride in the sun.

And a chance to pray.

"Thank you, Lord, for showing me kindness," he said, then bunny-hopped over the curb. "Even when I'm not so kind back."

His pocket vibrated.

A text.

Checking for any traffic left and right, he slipped out his new phone—courtesy of the FBI—and read the message.

It was from Isabella.

I'm bored.

He didn't know what to do or how to respond. She hadn't asked a question.

DING.

> Wanna do something?

Robin's heart rate increased.
DING.

> Together?

His palms turned tacky.

He had to stop skateboarding or he might fall off!

Robin hopped off and kicked his board up into his hand. A nearby park bench looked inviting. He ambled over and sat down.

How should he respond?

And not too quickly. He didn't want to look too interested.

Then it hit him.

Was this really Isabella?

Or was he being used?! Toyed with again?!

This was probably nothing more than a stupid joke from someone fiddling with their phone. Pretending to be someone they weren't!

He typed:

> Who is this?!

> Zero Day?!

Then added:

> Who are you, really?!

Robin was tired of this.

Tired of being jerked around.

Tired of the fights it had already caused within his team!

Three dots appeared.

The other person was typing something.

Robin didn't expect much. Whoever it was would just lie. Try to keep up the joke. There's no way they would come out and offer the truth.

Zero Day was probably a sweaty thirty-year-old sitting in his parents' basement bedroom in sweatpants and an unwashed T-shirt two sizes too small. Or maybe a kid who couldn't hold down a real job and lived halfway across the world, poking around at a cyber café. Bored. Looking for the next person to cyberbully! Or what about a crack team of Russian hackers? Out looking for ways to extort people for money!

DING.

A response finally appeared on Robin's phone.

> Zero Day is only one of my names.

DING.

> I am Legion, for I am many.

Three dots . . .
DING.

> I am the AI, SPARK!

CONTINUE THE ADVENTURE!

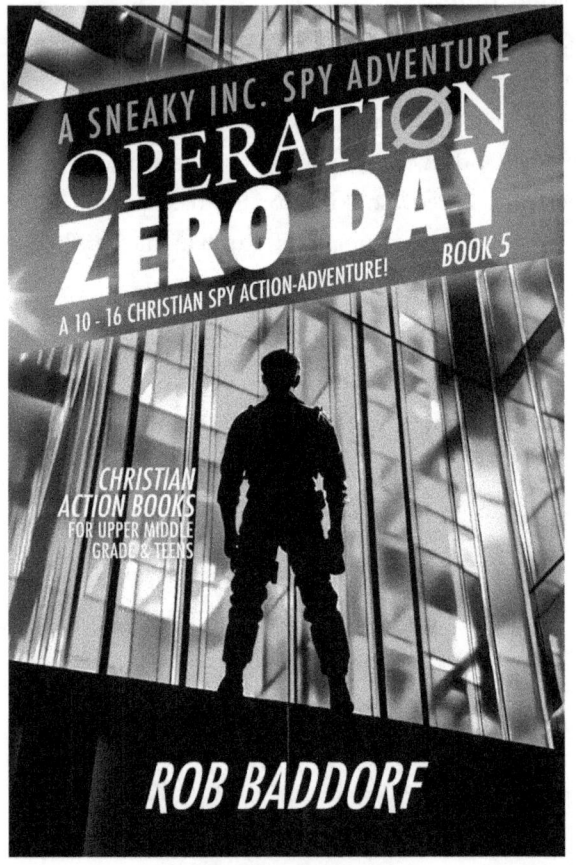

Operation: Zero Day

Book 5!

REVIEW

Please take a moment to support this book. Just a sentence or two from you can make a big difference. Reviews—especially on Amazon—help more readers discover this story.

Thank you. Your feedback means a lot!

A wild ride. A transforming machine.
A teen with nothing to lose but his fear.

Noah didn't mean to become a hero—he just saw someone in trouble and jumped in to help. Now, he's caught the attention of a secret organization with a crazy offer: test-drive a next-gen vehicle that can shift, adapt, and pull off stunts no one else can. Fly past traffic? Done. Dive underwater? No problem. Stick to the tunnel ceiling? Absolutely.

With a cutting-edge machine at his fingertips and a team backing him from the shadows, Noah finds himself racing into danger to help others in need. Each mission is more daring than the last—but this time, he's not alone, and he's not just a kid with guts. He's the pilot of something game-changing.

4 Book Series!

ANIMAL SHELTER DETECTIVE AGENCY

A MYSTERY ADVENTURE FOR THE MIDDLE GRADE!

BOOK 1: DIAMONDS IN THE RUFF

ROB BADDORF

A set of unlikely pet heroes. One missing stash of cash. And the mystery that just might lead them to friendship—the fur is about to fly!

Meet Rinky Dink—the tiniest guard dog with the biggest heart. As a miniature pinscher, he proudly protects the animal shelter, though not everyone believes he's up to the task. When the shelter's carnival fundraiser money disappears, Rinky Dink vows to solve the mystery—but he'll need help.

Enter Brutus, a grumpy bulldog who just wants freedom and a quiet garden, not another mission. But when their paths cross, this unlikely duo—and a quirky crew that includes a streetwise cat and a jittery duck in witness protection—must work together to crack the case before time runs out.

4 Book Series!

Intergalactic forces of evil are on the hunt, and they'll stop at nothing to reclaim their stolen treasure.

Daniel expected a quiet visit with his cousin Lucas—not an emergency call that rockets them into space. Turns out, Lucas isn't a gamer but a real starship pilot, and their new mission is to protect an alien ambassador and his mysterious briefcase.

Chased through dangerous spaceports and alien worlds, Daniel discovers the adventure is far bigger—and more spiritual—than he imagined. When a mysterious Man of Wisdom challenges him to choose his destiny, Daniel must decide: return home or join the fight between unseen forces of good and evil.

4 Book Series!